"You're perfec
with me, Giles."

He gave a bark of mirthless laughter. "I *used* to feel safe with you. But on a certain day over a year ago all that changed. Nowadays, your company, delightful though it may be, smacks of danger."

Eliza gave him a long, hard look. "I promise you. You're in no danger from me."

"You still don't get it. The danger lies with *my* baser impulses, not yours."

Eliza's patience suddenly deserted her. "That isn't really the problem, is it? Your ego just can't cope with the fact that I believed my sister instead of trusting you."

"For a while that was true. I wanted to wring your neck—and your twin's. But the danger I'm referring to is something rather different."

"I don't understand," she admitted.

"It's quite simple. My basic problem is that I want you."

Catherine George was born in Wales and, following her marriage to an engineer, lived in Brazil for eight years at a gold-mine site. Now her husband helps manage their household back in the U.K. so that Catherine can devote more time to her writing. They have two children—a daughter and a son—who share their mother's love of language. When not writing and reading, Catherine loves to cook, listen to opera, browse in antique shops and walk the Labrador.

Books by Catherine George

HARLEQUIN ROMANCE
3129—ARROGANT INTERLOPER
3147—A CIVILISED ARRANGEMENT
3177—UNLIKELY CUPID
3201—BRAZILIAN ENCHANTMENT
3236—LEADER OF THE PACK
3261—OUT OF THE STORM

HARLEQUIN PRESENTS
1016—LOVE LIES SLEEPING
1065—TOUCH ME IN THE MORNING
1152—VILLAIN OF THE PIECE
1184—TRUE PARADISE
1225—LOVEKNOT
1255—EVER SINCE EDEN
1321—COME BACK TO ME

AFTER THE BALL
Catherine George

Harlequin Books

TORONTO • NEW YORK • LONDON
AMSTERDAM • PARIS • SYDNEY • HAMBURG
STOCKHOLM • ATHENS • TOKYO • MILAN
MADRID • WARSAW • BUDAPEST • AUCKLAND

ISBN 0-373-17163-3

AFTER THE BALL

CHAPTER ONE

SHE knew every woman in the room envied her; not for the spectacular beaded dress and wild cascade of black curls, but because the man holding her close as they danced was the successful, wealthy birthday boy himself. Young and darkly attractive, her partner radiated the self-confidence of a man self-propelled at such speed from poverty to millionaire status that he was the current darling of the media.

The small hotel ballroom was packed wall-to-wall with guests invited to celebrate with Paul Wright, all of them enjoying themselves hugely at their host's expense as they danced to the music of a famous rock band. The one exception was the girl clamped so close to his chest that she could hardly breathe. The tightness of her dress had a lot to do with it, but by far her biggest stress factor was her partner, whose body language needed no translation. After the ball was over her host plainly expected to share her bed in the expensive room he'd reserved for her overnight stay.

Until five minutes earlier the band had been belting out its latest ear-splitting hit, with everyone bopping wildly to the music. Paul's covetous eyes had been so openly glued to the beads outlining the curves above her waist that she'd done her best to move as minimally as possible, short of standing still. But it came as no surprise to find him crushing her half to death once the music changed to its present moody, erotic beat. Her partner was making no bones about the fact that he fancied her like mad, and couldn't care less that everyone in the room knew he did.

'Have some more champagne,' he urged after a while.

Feeling like a lamb led to slaughter, she let him seat her on a small gilt sofa at their table, the touch of his fingers like a brand through the pink chiffon as he pulled her so close she might just as well have been on his lap.

Dry-mouthed with nerves, she would have preferred a glass of cold water to the champagne, but as the wine was the only thing on offer she sipped as sparingly as possible, and tried not to look at her watch.

'Having a good time?' whispered Paul, his breath scorching her ear.

'Wonderful,' she lied, smiling brightly. 'Brilliant party.'

Suddenly Paul jumped to his feet, waving animatedly as he spotted a man making his way towards them, sleek gold head high above the crowd.

'Over here! Good man—you made it,' Paul pumped the newcomer's hand, grinning in welcome. 'Miss Gemma Markham, Giles Randolph—the architect who masterminded my little place up the road. I think you two know each other.'

Stunned, her heart turning somersaults under the beads, she rose unsteadily to her feet, forcing a smile as she met the arrested blue gaze a good foot above her own.

'I know Gemma very well, Paul,' drawled Giles Randolph after a pause. He took her cold hand in his. 'I remember this lady when she wore braces on her teeth and the only man in her life was a pony.'

She withdrew her hand swiftly, fixing her eyes on the newcomer's black bow tie. 'Hello, Giles. What a surprise! I had no idea you two knew each other.'

Paul shot a puzzled look at her. 'I could have sworn I mentioned it the other night, darling. Don't you remember?'

'Oh—of course,' she said hastily, colouring. 'The champagne must be softening my brain.'

'I'd rather it softened your resistance!' Paul winked as he squeezed her waist. 'Look, sweetheart, I'll leave you two old mates together while I dash off and have a word with Cunningham and his lady—got to butter him up for a deal I've got cooking. Look after her for me, Giles. Won't be a tick.'

Wishing the floor would open up and swallow her, she gazed in despair after Paul as he laughed and joked his way across the room. In ominous silence Giles Randolph led her to join the dancers, steered her round for an obligatory minute or two, then collected two glasses of champagne from a passing waiter and, with surprising skill for someone of his stature, contrived to transfer himself and his unwilling partner from the ballroom to a deserted ante-room without attracting attention to their exit.

'We seem to have done this before,' he remarked and shut the door firmly behind him. He handed her one of the glasses, leaned against the door and drank some wine, his eyes like flint as they speared hers. 'So, Eliza Markham. You and Gemma up to your charming tricks again? Paul Wright's a tough customer, you stupid little idiot. What the hell do you think you're playing at?'

Eliza gave him a look of blazing dislike. 'You don't imagine this was my idea!'

'Since you're masquerading as Gemma, I suppose not. What brainless scheme has she cooked up this time?' His eyes ran over her from the tips of her satin shoes to the plunging neckline of her dress, his mouth twisting in distaste. 'Let's hope none of Paul's guests are acquainted with *both* the beautiful Markham twins. The resemblance is remarkable, I allow, Eliza, but to the informed eye there are certain outstanding differences.'

She ground her teeth impotently. 'You think I don't know that?'

'So. What happens when Paul finds out?'

Eliza suppressed a shudder. 'I'm supposed to make sure he doesn't.'

Giles strode across the room to stand over her. 'Even to the extent of making the supreme sacrifice, Eliza? The chap can't keep his hands off you. He quite obviously intends to round off his party by a session in bed—your bed,' he added menacingly.

She stifled a despairing groan. 'But Gem swore they weren't lovers, Giles, otherwise I'd never have agreed to take her place. She only met Paul a few days ago. She was modelling dresses outside his new restaurant in Wandsworth. He drove up in his Ferrari, they took one look at each other and, bingo, that was that. He's been giving her the rush treatment ever since, but she swore blind there'd been nothing between them other than kisses and—and so on, as yet.' Eliza thrust a hand through her expensive curls. 'In fact she's determined *not* to let him sleep with her, just to show him she's no pushover. I've never seen her in such a state over a man before.'

Giles took her by the shoulders and spun her round to face him. 'Then why the hell isn't she here tonight?'

'She got stung by a wasp.'

He stared incredulously. 'And that kept her away?'

Eliza shrugged free of his grasp. 'Yes! Wild horses couldn't have managed it, but the wasp did. I went up to town to a sale at Sotheby's yesterday and had supper with her afterwards. She kept on and on about Paul and the party and the dress she'd bought, then halfway through watering the pansies in her window-box she screamed her head off and dropped the can. A wasp had stung her on one of the main veins in the armpit and in seconds she began to swell up, nose, eyelids, earlobes all twice their size, and her skin striped red and white like a strawberry sundae. Luckily Tom Metcalfe—her landlord—was on hand. He rushed us at top speed to St Mary's but her tongue was almost choking her by the time we got there.' Eliza shuddered at the memory. 'I was so frightened I was ready to promise anything in the state she was in.'

Giles swore under his breath. 'Even to the extent of agreeing to take her place tonight, no doubt.'

'Yes,' she said flatly. 'Even that.'

'So. With your invaluable help Paul is now more firmly enmeshed in the Markham spell than ever, except he hasn't a clue it's Eliza he's lusting after at this precise moment in time, and not Gemma.' Giles's scrutiny travelled over her with insulting deliberation again, the scorn in his eyes opening old wounds she'd been so sure were long since healed. 'I assume that's Gemma's dress?'

'Of course it is,' she snapped, flushing. 'I can hardly breathe in the wretched thing, and I've never worn pink since——' She looked away, biting her lip.

His mouth tightened. 'Surely Paul's noticed that you're rounder in certain areas than your twin?'

Eliza glared at him malevolently. 'If he has, he certainly doesn't find it off-putting.'

'Which was blindingly obvious to everyone in the room! So what happens at midnight, Cinderella? That provocative dress won't change to rags, but Paul Wright is certain to want to dispense with it—along with anything else you happen to be wearing.'

'Don't be disgusting,' she hissed, trying to hide her blind panic at the truth of what he was saying. But Paul Wright had been behaving like a victor with the spoils all evening. Giles, she knew only too well, had hit the nail very firmly on the head.

'Can you go through with it?' he went on relentlessly. 'Are you prepared to surrender your all to Paul Wright just to keep his engine running for your twin?'

Suddenly Eliza bitterly regretted the lobster she'd eaten earlier. Stomach churning, she stared down at her clenched hands, trying to find words to beg Giles for help.

'Unless, of course,' said Giles ruthlessly, 'you're quite happy with the idea. Paul Wright's young, successful, wealthy. An aphrodisiac combination. Perhaps you fancy him for yourself.'

Eliza turned on him like a tigress. 'How dare you?'

'I dare,' he retorted, advancing on her, 'for your family's sake, because your brother is my oldest friend. Rob isn't here, so it falls to me to act in his place.' He paused, eyeing her implacably. 'But before I offer help I want to know whether you really want delivery from Paul—or not.'

Eliza's fingernails bit into the skin of her palms. 'Of course I do,' she said with passion, when she could trust herself to speak. 'For one thing I never poach on any woman's preserves, let alone Gemma's. And for another it's not my style to jump into bed with a man I've just met, Paul Wright—and all his material attributes—included.'

'So ask me to help you, then,' he said very softly, holding her eyes captive.

Eliza tried to look away, but failed. She ran the tip of her tongue round suddenly dry lips, trying to find the hated words. 'Can you help me—please, Giles?' she blurted at last.

'If I do,' he said, moving closer, 'I expect a reward.'

Eliza stood very still as he reached out to grasp her by the shoulders, the beads over her breasts glittering with her hurried breathing as he pulled her against him. She closed her eyes tightly in a vain attempt to hide her body's traitorous response to the contact, then gasped as his mouth met hers in a kiss of such length and intensity that her knees were knocking together by the time he thrust her away from him.

'I think I deserved that—to start with.' He stepped back, eyeing her incensed face with sarcastic pleasure. 'All right, then, Eliza, let's think. No doubt you're staying here tonight?'

She nodded, breathing hard as she fought for composure. 'Paul booked a room for Gem.'

Giles eyed her for some time in nerve-jangling silence.

'So what can I *do*?' burst out Eliza at last.

'Go and powder your nose, or whatever, then go back to Paul. When I feed you the cue, act up for all you're worth.'

'What's your plan?' she said suspiciously.

'No point in telling you or it'll look rehearsed. Come on.' He took her by the arm and hustled her from the room. 'Off you go. I'll come to Paul's table after a suitable interval.'

Eliza pulled herself together, put all thoughts of Giles's kiss from her mind, and concentrated on giving an Oscar-winning performance when she rejoined Paul and his friends. She talked and laughed as though she were having the time of her life as Paul grew more and more possessive, his arm tightening about her waist, every look, every gesture indicating all too clearly exactly what he had in mind after the ball was over. Thankful that Paul was the host, and obliged to stay until at least some of his guests departed, Eliza forced herself to play up to him for all she was worth now she knew help was at hand. She leaned against him pliantly, returned his burning looks in kind, doing her best to behave as she imagined Gemma would have done, while underneath it all every nerve was stretched to its limit as she kept an eye out for Giles. At screaming point by the time she spotted his bright hair, visible as usual above everyone else's in the room, Eliza felt her heart skip a beat at the grave look on his face.

'Where've you been? Come and have a drink,' urged Paul, waving a hand to a nearby chair, but Giles shook his head.

'I won't actually, old chap. Afraid I'm the bearer of bad tidings.'

Paul's sharp eyes narrowed. 'What's up?'

Giles turned to Eliza. 'I was at the desk when a phone call came for you. I had a quick word with the manager and volunteered to break the news. Your sister's ill. She's been rushed into St Mary's, Paddington.'

Eliza leapt to her feet, a hand to her mouth. 'Oh, no!'

Paul put a protective arm round her. 'Don't worry, I'll drive you there right now——'

'Bad idea, old chap,' warned Giles. 'You've probably had a glass too many to drive. Besides, you can't desert your guests. I'll give Gemma a lift to town. You hang on here. She can ring you later.'

Paul Wright, looking like a tiger balked of its prey, began to protest violently, but Eliza put a hand on his arm.

'*Please*—darling. Giles is right.' She took her courage in both hands and reached up to kiss him full on the mouth. 'I'll ring you when I get there. See you soon. Promise.'

Paul Wright crushed her in his arms and returned the kiss in full measure, oblivious of curious eyes on all sides as he released a scarlet Eliza with a reluctance he made no effort to hide.

'Get a move on, Gemma,' ordered Giles brusquely. 'Run up and get your things. We'd better be off.'

The fraught few minutes between Giles's announcement and actually getting into his car brought Eliza to the point of hysteria. Almost weak with relief, she gave a final wave to Paul, then slumped in her seat, feeling limp, as Giles drove off at top speed to emphasise the urgency of their mission to the man watching them out of sight.

'Ugh!' she shuddered, as they sped along deserted roads. 'I will never, ever let Gem persuade me to do that again. It was utterly horrible. I *loathed* having to lie like that.'

'Then why the hell agree to such a stupid escapade in the first place?' he snapped. 'Besides, as far as the last bit's concerned it was the truth. Your sister *was* taken ill, and she did go to St Mary's. When Gemma recovers she can just switch the experience to you.' He laughed shortly. 'Mind you, Eliza, it's to be hoped her illness doesn't take too much weight off her or Paul's likely to smell a rat. Frankly I'm amazed he didn't remark on the improvement in your vital statistics tonight.'

Eliza sent a look of black dislike at his profile. 'As a matter of fact he did. But he doesn't know Gem that well yet, so I just said I'd put on weight since I bought the dress.'

'And he swallowed it?'

'Yes,' she said angrily. 'He did.'

'Even so, you'd better warn Gemma to stuff herself with calories before she sees him again.'

'She'd love to. It's only Gem's career that keeps her to a strict diet, believe me!'

Giles sent her a satirical glance. 'So if you lived on lettuce leaves and fresh air you'd look as fragile as she does, I take it?'

'I doubt it,' she snapped. 'It would take more than a few lettuce leaves to make *me* look fragile, even if I had the least desire to do so, which I don't. My career requires stamina, not fragility.'

'Temper, temper!' he mocked. 'No need to be defensive about your attractions, Eliza. Paul certainly found them potent enough. He was quite obviously at boiling point by the time I, like the cavalry, finally arrived. And frankly you seemed so receptive of his attentions that I wondered for a moment if my intervention was necessary after all.'

Eliza gritted her teeth. 'To use your phrase, Giles, I was just keeping his engine running for Gemma. Now can we *please* drop the subject?'

'By all means. Who am I to expect gratitude—or any other sincere emotion where you're concerned?' he said harshly. 'Take a nap. Perhaps you'll wake up in more gracious mood.'

Eliza, burningly conscious that thanks were necessary, utterly failed to get the words out. Just finding herself alone with Giles Randolph again was too much for nerves already taxed to the utmost all evening. Fighting the urge to cry her eyes out, she clenched them shut and pretended she was asleep, then sat up abruptly minutes later as the car came to a halt.

'Why have we stopped?' she asked suspiciously. 'Have you run out of petrol?'

'No,' said Giles, hauling her out of the car.

Eliza stared blankly at a tall building outlined against the starlit sky, and situated, as far as she could tell, in the middle of nowhere. 'What are we doing here?' she demanded, suddenly afraid.

'This is my house.' Giles stooped to take her suitcase from the back then ushered her up a short flight of steps to the main door.

Eliza rounded on him. 'I thought you were driving me to London!'

'Why?' Giles unlocked his door and switched on some lights. 'Neither of us lives there.'

'No, but Gem does. You said you were taking me to her!'

'Since Gemma fully expected you to be staying overnight at the Manor Hotel, what's the point?' Giles yawned suddenly and thrust her into the sparsely furnished main room of what was obviously a barn conversion, with the posts and trusses of the original structure exposed in all their glory. 'I've just got back from a trip to the States and felt obliged to put in an appearance at Paul's thrash, but now I'm tired, jet-lagged and frankly irritable. I'm in no mood to drive to London or anywhere else so you'll just have to stay here overnight. I'll take you home tomorrow.'

Eliza eyed him militantly. 'Won't Marina object to an unexpected guest?'

Giles's mouth tightened. 'No. Your family grapevine's failed you, Eliza. I'd have thought you'd heard. Marina and I split up recently—very recently.'

Eliza was at a loss for something to say. Giles's expression forbade comment. Yet it seemed rude to make none at all. If only she could have driven herself to the party, she thought despairingly, none of this would have been necessary. But she'd had to travel by train in her role as Gemma because her twin flatly refused to learn to drive.

'I'm sorry,' she said after an awkward pause. 'Rob said you'd moved last time I spoke to him, but——'

'But he left out the reason for the sudden change of scene,' said Giles evenly.

'Yes, he did.'

He moved towards her, halting abruptly as she backed away. 'What the hell's the matter now?' His eyes gleamed with sudden derision. 'Ah, I see! You're worried about spending the night alone with me. Surely you're not worried about propriety, Eliza?'

'No. It's not propriety that worries me,' she said bluntly.

His face hardened. 'You're still Rob's sister. Is it likely I'd rescue you from the clutches of one man, only to leap on you myself?'

Her colour rose at the sarcasm in the deep, resonant voice. 'No, I suppose not,' she muttered, her eyes falling.

He smiled sardonically. 'But it occurred to you that I might just indulge in a little retaliation for the treatment you dished out to me last time we met!'

'Something like that, yes.'

Giles turned away wearily. 'I don't know what I ever did to earn your opinion of me, Eliza, but don't worry. You can rest in peace under my roof tonight. Or any other night, if it comes to that.'

'I'm relieved to hear it.' She felt suddenly guilty, and resented it. 'But you certainly don't have to drive me anywhere tomorrow, except to the nearest station. I'll go up to London to Gem the same way I came. By train.'

Giles shrugged. 'As you like. You're shivering. Shall I switch on the heating?'

'No, don't bother. I'm not cold exactly. It's just reaction. I was on edge every minute of that hateful charade tonight.'

'Have a brandy.'

'No, thanks.' She forced a smile. 'Would it be too much trouble to ask for tea, Giles?'

'I think I can manage that.'

'And may I ring Gemma, please?'

'By all means. Prime her with all the details, then tell *her* to ring the ardent Paul.' Giles looked down his formidable nose at her. 'I might even have a word with her myself, tell her to make sure she never dreams up anything so bird-brained again——'

'No, thank you! I'll deal with Gemma.' She paused. 'Unless, of course, you *want* to talk to her.'

He shrugged and picked up her suitcase and a mobile phone. 'Not particularly. I'll show you to the guest-room. You can talk to Gemma up there in private. Only don't take all night.'

'I'll pay for the call, of course,' said Eliza, following up to a gallery which ran round the upper half of the main room.

Giles shot her a scathing look as he opened a bedroom door. 'Don't be offensive.' He dumped her suitcase down beside the bed, waved a hand at the door leading to the bathroom, then slammed the door behind him, leaving her alone.

For a moment Eliza's curiosity about her surroundings overcame the urge to phone Gemma. The room was oddly impersonal, nor was the adjoining bathroom in the least sybaritic. But it contained a mirror, and one look at her reflection decided her to remove her elaborate Gemma-make-up before she did anything else at all. She splashed cold water on her face vigorously once it was clean, then attacked the wilting curls with a dampened brush until her hair looked normal again. At last, feeling more like herself, she sat on the bed and dialled Gemma's number.

Her sister answered so quickly it was obvious she'd been wide awake. Brushing aside Eliza's enquiries about her state of health, Gemma fired a fusillade of questions before her sister could get another word in.

'Oh, do shut up for a minute, Gem,' ordered Eliza irritably, then gave a short, succinct account of the evening, ending with an instruction to Gemma to make the required phone call to Paul at the Manor Hotel. 'I should give it half an hour or so,' she advised. 'The way Giles drives, that should be about right.'

'Oh, Liza,' groaned Gemma, horrified. 'Why did it have to be Giles, of all people! You must have loathed asking him for help. Besides, it never occurred to me that Paul might have, well——'

'Fancied a red-hot session in bed to round off the evening?'

'Don't be coarse!'

'Have you any *idea* what a terrible strain it was for me all evening, fending the man off?'

'Sorry,' sighed Gemma forlornly, then gave a little shriek. 'What do you mean, strain? Didn't you want to fend him off?'

'Of course I did. The man's your property, idiot, not to mention a complete stranger to me. Besides, Paul Wright may be sexy and charming and utterly perfect as far as you're concerned, but he's not *my* cup of tea.'

Gemma, far from being reassured by this, flew up in arms in defence of Paul Wright's attractions, unable to credit the fact that Eliza was immune to them. Eliza cut her off mid-flow, took her again through the salient points of the evening, learned with relief that her twin was restored to near-normal looks again, then finished off with Giles's advice to Gemma on stuffing herself with every fattening food she could think of before meeting Paul again.

'He definitely noticed my more generous dimensions,' warned Eliza. 'I had to fib about putting on weight since buying the dress. I just loved telling so many lies,' she added bitterly. 'This is the last time, Gem. No more switching. Ever.'

'Tell her she'll have me to answer to if she suggests it again,' ordered a voice from the door.

'My host has come to cut me off,' said Eliza, eyeing Giles coldly. 'Make the phone call, Gemma, then get a good night's sleep and make sure you put off seeing Paul for a day or two until you look human again. Bye.'

'Your phone bills must be astronomical,' said Giles, looking at his watch.

'I was on the phone for exactly ten minutes! I spent some time tidying myself up before I rang Gemma,' she said, offended.

'So I see,' said Giles, surveying the results. 'Incidentally, does Gemma realise that it was my intervention that saved your virtue?'

'I told her you interfered, yes,' she snapped, then bit her lip. 'I beg your pardon. That was uncalled for. I—I really do appreciate your help.'

Giles looked sceptical. 'If that's true let me give you some advice, Eliza. Don't play any more little games like tonight's escapade. I might not be on hand to rescue you another time.'

'There won't be another time,' she said, keeping calm with enormous effort. 'I've managed my life perfectly well up to now without your help, Giles Randolph. I'll make very sure you're not forced to put yourself out on my behalf again!'

CHAPTER TWO

THE atmosphere dropped to sub-zero as Giles led the way downstairs to the room below. He waved Eliza to a leather chesterfield sofa vast enough to suit its surroundings, then strode off through a door at the far end, presently reappearing with a tray which he set down on a low table in front of her.

'Your tea,' he said curtly. He went over to a side-table to mix himself a whisky and soda, then settled himself in a large chair upholstered in comfortably shabby velvet. 'Would you like something to eat?'

'No, thanks. But I'm grateful for the tea. I don't think I'll ever drink champagne again.'

'Why not?'

'Guilt association from tonight.' She looked up to meet his expressionless blue gaze. 'It went against the grain to deceive Paul Wright like that. He's not the jumped-up oik I expected. Rather to my surprise, I quite liked him.'

'As much as Gemma does?'

'No, of course not. But I was prejudiced by what I'd read about him in the Press. In other circumstances he'd have been pleasant enough company, but, as it was, the evening was sheer hell from start to finish.'

'He's no fool, young Paul—owning a chain of fast-food restaurants at the ripe old age of thirty isn't bad for a boy who started out in his teens washing dishes in a West End hotel.'

Eliza nodded, relieved to discuss a reasonably neutral subject. 'Pity about the excruciating name, though. Was it his idea to call his eating places "the Wright Stuff"?'

'Absolutely. Paul masterminds every single detail. We had one or two confrontations when he tried to do the same over the plans for his extension.' Giles smiled in the superior way she remembered of old. 'So far I'm the victor—possibly because I'm twice his size, but more probably because the annexe I designed for the Manor Hotel won an award. Paul's impressed by awards.' He waved a hand at the lofty, spacious room. 'Forget this place is mine for a minute, and give me your opinion of my new home, Eliza.'

She ran her eyes over the white-emulsioned walls, oatmeal carpet and curtains, the outsize leather furniture, the surprising dearth of ornaments.

He gestured impatiently. 'Don't be nervous, Eliza. Be as honest as you like. I value a free opinion from an interior designer—even one of the fledgeling variety like you.'

'Not so much of the fledgeling these days, Giles,' she contradicted tartly. 'I know quite enough about the business to give the thumbs-down to all this porridge. These glorious beams need drama and touches of colour here and there to complement them, for a start.'

Giles shrugged. 'The carpets and curtains were surplus to requirements at the Manor Hotel. I made the move from Oxford so suddenly I snapped them up so I could get in here as quickly as possible.' His mouth twisted. 'At the time I wasn't concerned with aesthetics.'

There was an awkward little silence.

'I'm sorry,' said Eliza, clearing her throat. 'About Marina, I mean.'

'Are you?'

'Yes. Is that so hard to believe?'

Giles smiled derisively. 'Frankly, yes. I still bear the scars from our last encounter, Eliza.'

'Really?' She laughed a little. 'How strange. I'd forgotten all about it.'

'You're lying!'

'If I do remember,' she said carefully, 'it's only because it was Rob's wedding day.'

'Of course,' he agreed suavely. 'What other importance could you attach to it?' He sprang to his feet, and Eliza shrank back into her corner of the large settee, feeling foolish when Giles merely went over to the drinks tray to pour himself another whisky.

'Are you sure I can't give you anything?' he asked over his shoulder.

'Yes, thank you. The tea was quite enough.'

He turned, studying her in silence for a while. 'Rob tells me you're doing very well at your firm for a relative beginner.'

Eliza shrugged, ignoring the hint of patronage. 'Actually I'm enjoying a modest success—recommended by word of mouth, and all that. But I can give you some advice for free right now. Keep the carpet and buy a rug or two for colour. But those curtains are gross. And I haven't seen the other upstairs rooms, but the guest-room's like an anchorite's cell, Giles.'

He smiled indifferently. 'Adequate for the purpose. Now I'm on the loose again, as it were, I like my female guests to be comfortable, but not so comfortable that they outstay their welcome.'

Eliza flushed, and looked at her watch. 'I see. Well, in that case I'll bid you goodnight. Not that there's any possibility of outstaying *my* welcome, of course.' She got up, eyeing him with hostility. 'Because there was never any welcome for me in the first place, was there?'

Giles moved towards her in a way which made it difficult for her to hold her ground. 'Does that surprise you?' he demanded.

'No. What does surprise me is your rescue attempt,' she said bluntly. 'Why did you feel obliged to play knight errant, Giles?'

'I told you,' he said shortly. 'Because you're Rob's sister. He'd do the same for me.'

'You don't have a sister!'

'For which,' said Giles succinctly, 'I'm profoundly grateful.'

'So why didn't you leave me to stew in my own juice tonight?'

'At this moment I wish I had!' he said irritably, then gave a mammoth yawn.

Eliza bit her lip as she noticed the dark shadows under his eyes. 'I'm sorry to have given you so much trouble. And I haven't been sufficiently grateful, I know. But I am, Giles. Truly.'

He made no response, his eyes on the hair which hung, dark and glossily straight now to her shoulders. 'You look more like the Eliza I remember now,' he remarked. 'Those wild curls of yours almost had me fooled at first.'

Eliza looked away to hide a *frisson* of reaction to his tone. 'Not my style at all. Gem had a perm for a recent shoot in South Beach, Miámi, so she packed me off to her hairdresser to get mine done to match this morning—yesterday morning, really. Glory, I'm so tired I can't tell what day it is.'

'That makes two of us. What time do you want breakfast?'

'Never eat it.' Something in his eyes sent Eliza hurrying towards the stairs, starting up them at such speed that the high slender heel of one of Gemma's satin evening shoes skidded over a polished wooden tread and sent her reeling backwards. Giles fielded her neatly and scooped her up against his chest.

'Careful,' he said very softly. 'If you're that tired I'll give you a lift.'

Eliza, knowing it was useless to struggle, held herself rigid in his arms until he set her on her feet on the upper gallery.

'That was entirely unnecessary,' she said stiffly.

'Possibly, but highly enjoyable. For me, at least.' His eyes travelled over her in a slow, analytical scrutiny she resented fiercely.

'I wish you wouldn't keep eyeing me as if I were a specimen on a slide!'

'A very beautiful specimen,' Giles assured her. 'Actually I was thinking you'd be unwise to wear that dress again, Eliza.'

'If I were wise I'd never have worn it in the first place!' She sighed dispiritedly. 'Besides, I'm not likely to wear the wretched thing again. It's Gemma's. She's the glamorous one. Not me.'

Giles frowned. 'What the hell are you talking about? You and Gemma are mirror images of each other for a start—those slanting eyes and that mouth . . .' He paused, eyeing the feature in question so long that she became restive. 'Admittedly,' he went on, 'the resemblance stops at that point, mainly because Gemma makes her living from her looks, while you use your brain, taste, skill, and whatever else an interior designer needs to be successful. And,' he added, his eyes dropping deliberately to her neckline, 'when it comes to choice, my own preference lies with curves rather than bones. Any day.' Abruptly he opened the guest-room door and gave her a push. 'Go to bed, Eliza, before I do something I'll regret—again.'

Eliza's brows rose in derision. 'You, Giles? Regret anything? Surely not!'

His face hardened. 'Since you ask, I'm referring to the last time we met, when I laid myself open to a form of humiliation never experienced at a woman's hands before—or since.'

'Oh, that,' said Eliza airily. She stopped short, swallowing at the look on Giles's face as he barred the way to his guest-room door.

'Yes—that!' he said through his teeth, and jerked her into his arms, tightening them cruelly.

Eliza gasped, appalled at her uncontrollable surge of response. 'Let me go, Giles—please.'

'Not yet, I think,' he said harshly.

Eliza began to fight, but Giles held her fast.

'I see you remember the incident quite well, after all!'

'All right, all right,' she said wearily, giving up the struggle. 'Of course I remember.' Her eyes met his. 'But if the memory still rankles so much, why did you decide to help me out tonight?'

'For old times' sake, I suppose. I was very fond of the *young* Eliza.' He stepped back, releasing her. 'In any case, I had no idea help was needed at first. But once Paul introduced you as Gemma I felt I'd better do something—even at the risk of your ingratitude for my interference,' he added cuttingly.

Eliza thrust a hand through her hair wearily. 'I can't go on apologising, Giles. Now if you'll just let me pass I'll go to bed, and in the morning I'll leave as early as possible and make sure our paths never cross again.'

'As you've done so efficiently ever since the wedding,' he commented grimly. 'You've been conspicuously absent from any gatherings at Rob's place whenever I was invited—including the farewell party before he left for New Zealand with Sally.'

'I was present at the private family dinner,' said Eliza defensively. 'Rob understood about the other times. I—I explained that you and I just don't get on these days.'

'Which led to some pretty awkward questions from him about what I'd done to offend you,' said Giles acidly. 'But don't worry. I was the perfect gentleman. I didn't let on that *you* were the offender, not I.'

Her eyes flashed. 'Was I really? I remember things rather differently. Would Rob have been pleased to know you tried to seduce his sister, I wonder?'

'Seduce?' Giles gave a scornful bark of laughter. 'If there was any seduction going on, Eliza, I wasn't the only one involved.'

She shrugged impatiently, suddenly too tired to argue. 'Look, I didn't ask to come here, Giles, and I'll leave as soon as I can in the morning, but in the meantime can I *please* go to bed?'

Giles moved away from the door, abruptly very formal as he held it open for her. 'By all means. Goodnight, Eliza.'

She brushed past him, stumbling a little in her haste to escape. Giles put out a hand meant to steady her, but suddenly she was in his arms, his mouth meeting hers in an engulfing kiss which she responded to helplessly. She leaned against him, defenceless, her lips parting to the urgency of his hard, seeking mouth, the blood pounding through her veins in response, rendering her oblivious to everything other than the sheer physical delight of the moment. Then the caress of his long fingers on her breasts brought her down to earth in a rush, and she pushed fiercely against his restraining arms.

Giles released her at once, his cool tone belying the molten look in his eyes. 'Even St George probably demanded some kind of reward for slaying the dragon, Eliza.'

She scrubbed at her trembling mouth, then without a word she went into Giles Randolph's guest-room and slammed the door in his face. She stripped off the offending dress and hurled it away from her in disgust, then hurried through her preparations for bed, desperate to blot out the evening in sleep.

But sleep played hard to get. Giles's lovemaking had resurrected all the feelings she'd tried so long to damp down, and behind her closed eyelids the scene at Rob's wedding played itself over and over again, like an endless video-tape which refused to switch off.

The speeches had been over and the wedding cake cut, and the guests had been milling between dining-room and ballroom as the second phase of the celebrations got under way. The orchestra was playing something slow and dreamy in deference to members of the older generation, and Eliza, in yards of pink silk, with rosebuds in her upswept hair, had drifted

towards Giles, her eyes glittering with an invitation
he had answered by taking her in his arms and holding
her close as they revolved slowly to the music.

Eliza turned over restlessly in bed as she remembered the blaze in Giles's eyes when she'd reached on
tiptoe to whisper in his ear, suggesting they steal away
to his hotel room upstairs for a while.

'My *room*, Eliza?' His hand crushed hers as he
stared down at her.

'Why not?' She smiled dreamily. 'I'm very tired,
and it's so hot in here. I just want a few minutes'
peace. No one will notice us go. And even if they do
it won't cause comment. We're old friends, after all.'

Giles, utterly magnificent in his formal wedding
gear, gazed down into the flushed, cajoling face.
'There's a drawback, Eliza. At this moment friendly
doesn't describe the way I feel.'

Her eyes, skilfully accented for the occasion,
widened artfully. 'Why? What have I done?'

'I mean,' he said through his teeth, 'that there's
nothing platonic about what's suddenly going on between us—and you know it.'

Eliza dropped her eyes and moved closer, trusting
in the contact of their bodies to speak for her. And
it did. His face suddenly colourless, Giles managed
to manoeuvre them next to an emergency exit as the
music finished, and under cover of the applause he
drew her through the concealed door and up a flight
of back stairs to his room on the first floor.

Triumphant and breathless, Eliza whirled to face
him, challenge in every line of her as Giles leaned
against the door he'd just locked.

'Well?' he demanded. 'Here we are, and there's the bed. So if you want a rest, by all means make use of it.'

'I don't *really* want a rest, Giles!' She gave him a smile as old as Eve. 'I'm a big girl now, not just Rob's little sister, in case you hadn't noticed.'

'I'd noticed,' he said grimly, his eyes glittering darkly as they watched her revolve, laughing, her arms widespread.

'Don't you think I make a nice bridesmaid, Giles? You didn't kiss me in the vestry when everyone else did. Why not?'

'I had my reasons.'

'Didn't you want to kiss me?'

At which point Giles reached the end of his tether. He lunged away from the door and caught her in his arms, kissing her so hard that her whole body exulted at his ferocity.

'I didn't kiss you,' he said hoarsely against her open, gasping mouth, 'because from the moment I set eyes on you today I knew that if I ever started I might not stop.' And then there were no more words as he began a sustained assault on Eliza's reeling senses, wooing her with lips and hands and half-stifled endearments. Rosebuds scattered in all directions as she collapsed on the bed beneath him in a welter of rustling pink silk and tumbling hair, their agonised breathing the only sound in the room as Giles tore off his morning coat and cravat, his mouth moving hungrily over her face and throat as he dispensed with his shirt.

Eliza forgot everything: the wedding, her parents, Gemma, the entire world, as she locked her arms round Giles's neck and gave him back kiss for kiss, glorying in the touch of his hands as he freed her breasts from the low neckline of her dress. She gave a strangled cry as his mouth closed on a pointing red nipple, arrows of fire shooting through her body as she clutched his head closer and arched her back in an ecstasy of response.

But as Giles rose to kneel over her, stripped to the waist, his bright hair falling over his tense, passion-blank face, Eliza's conscience prodded her, recalling her to the purpose which had brought her there in the first place. She rallied her disintegrating self-control and pushed him away with a scornful little laugh which took him so much by surprise that she managed to slip from the bed and escape his seeking hands.

A shiver ran through her now as she remembered the outrage masking the bitter hurt on his face when she'd smiled in fake triumph to hide the tumult shaking her to pieces deep inside.

'Time we got back to the others, I think,' she'd said sweetly, and Giles had lain like a half-naked statue, his eyes burning with a look she'd never been able to forget.

'Just be glad it was me,' he'd said very softly, in a tone which had turned her blood to ice. 'If you're wise you'll never try a trick like that again. Another man might not be so forbearing—you hellish little teaser.'

Eliza slept for a while at last, but not for long. She woke up with a start, feeling wretched, and raced to the bathroom to part with the dinner Paul Wright had paid so much for earlier. Shivering and gasping, she crawled back into bed afterwards, but not to sleep. To her intense misery the episode was repeated at intervals until the dawn chorus tuned up, by which time

Eliza felt half-dead. She lay motionless, watching the early May sunlight grow brighter, almost too feeble to respond when a quiet tap sounded on her door.

Giles, immensely tall in a long, dark dressing-gown, strode quickly to the bed when he saw her ashen face. 'Hell, Eliza, you look like death. I heard you in the night a couple of times, but I didn't think you'd welcome an enquiry as to what was wrong.'

'It was half a dozen times, to be exact,' she said hoarsely. 'Must be something I ate. Sorry I woke you.'

'I wasn't asleep.' He turned away. 'I'll boil some water.'

She brightened. 'For tea?'

'No. To drink. You're probably dehydrated.'

Too dispirited to argue, Eliza lay, exhausted, dozing a little until Giles returned, looking dauntingly immaculate in a dark blue polo shirt and pale chinos.

'Up you come,' he ordered.

'No!' Eliza clutched the covers to her throat. 'I can manage.'

'My dear girl,' he said scathingly, 'I won't seethe with lust at the sight of your nightgown, I promise.'

'No, you won't,' she agreed, and sat up, wincing as a spasm of pain shot through her head.

He let out a bark of laughter as he stacked the pillows behind her. 'You actually went off for your night of sin armed with a T-shirt begging the beholder to save the planet?'

'Since it's the sort of thing I normally wear to bed, yes,' she replied with dignity, pushing her hair behind her ears. 'I was not, if you remember, anticipating any "sin".'

'So you told me. Though frankly, Eliza,' he added, as he poured water into a glass, 'you were damned naïve not to.'

'I realise that now,' she said bitterly, and drained the glass in such rash haste that she stiffened. 'Could you go away, please, Giles? If my stomach decides to revolt again I'll need privacy.'

'All right, relax—I'll come back in half an hour to see how you are.'

Left alone Eliza lay perfectly still, fighting her digestive system into submission. It was a long time before she felt confident enough to crawl shakily from the bed. She staggered to the bathroom to brush her teeth and wash her pallid face, gave a few dispirited swipes at her hair with a brush then went back to bed, feeling very sorry for herself.

'I won't say you look better, exactly,' Giles commented when he returned to check up on her. 'But I think there's a marginal improvement.'

'Probably because I had a wash.' She shuddered. 'I'm a sight.'

'No. Just fragile this morning, like it or not.' Giles gave her an impersonal smile. 'Right, then, Eliza, you can have some tea now.'

'Thank you. Then I must go.'

He frowned impatiently. 'Don't be silly. You're going nowhere until you're better.'

'But, Giles——'

'Don't argue! Just relax and try to get some rest.'

She subsided mutinously. 'I must be putting you out, Giles. Don't you have plans for today?'

'None,' he assured her. 'I'm going out for half an hour after I bring your tea, but otherwise my time's my own. Mrs Treasure, the aptly named lady who "does" for me, stocked me up with food yesterday, so we shan't starve.'

Eliza shuddered. 'Don't mention food!'

'You may feel differently in a while. Drink your tea, ring Gemma, then try to sleep.'

Alone in the quiet house, Eliza drained the teapot dry before she felt up to ringing her sister. Gemma expressed horrified sympathy for Eliza's state of health, asked some guarded questions about Giles, then plunged into a panegyric of praise for Paul, who'd been so sweet to her when she'd telephoned the night before. By a stroke of luck he was off to Cornwall for a couple of days for the opening of his latest restaurant, and full of apologies for not being able to meet Gemma until the middle of the week.

'So you see, it all fits in beautifully,' finished Gemma with satisfaction. 'You've been such an angel, Eliza. So has Tom. He's been feeding me so well that by Wednesday I'll be back to normal and Paul will never be any the wiser.'

'I hope you're right.'

'Don't worry! Just get well as quickly as you can.' Gemma paused. 'I feel terrible about all this, Liza. Not just because you're ill, but—well, being trapped with Giles Randolph on top of it.'

'If it hadn't been for Giles I might have had a lot more to contend with than a mere stomach upset,' Eliza pointed out, and said goodbye rather out of patience with her twin.

To her surprise she fell asleep almost at once. When she woke, feeling almost human again, Giles was standing in the open doorway, looking at her.

'Hello,' he said casually. 'Better?'

Eliza heaved herself up against the pillows, her recovery advanced enough to leave room in her mind for embarrassment about the way they'd parted the night before. 'Yes. Thank you.' Her eyes slid from his. 'It feels late. Have I slept long?'

'Hours.' He strolled to the bed. 'It's three in the afternoon. I've been up to check on you once or twice but you were out for the count.'

She bit her lip. 'Sorry. I rang Gem, then went out like a light.'

'Best thing you could do, in the circumstances. Now,' he went on briskly. 'How about something to eat?'

'No, thank you.'

'More tea, then. I'll bring it up.'

'Certainly not! I'll come down. I'm perfectly all right now—well, not perfectly, but enough to get up and dress.'

'Good, because there's a lady waiting to meet you downstairs.'

Eliza glared at him, incensed. 'Visitors? You said——'

'I know what I said. Ten minutes,' he said inexorably, and went out, closing the door.

Heaping curses on Giles Randolph's head, Eliza got out of bed, feeling a great deal better, but in no condition to cope with a female visitor, especially one of the expensive, glossy kind Giles normally favoured. Wishing she'd been able to steal away at dawn before he woke, she had a hasty bath, pulled on a loose navy jersey, and made the gratifying discovery that her jeans were easier to zip up after the rigours of the night. She brushed her hair, smoothed a trace of colour into her pale cheeks to offset the draining effect

of the sweater, then slid on navy leather loafers and
went on leaden feet from the room. She paused at the
head of the stairs to peer down into the room, but
there was no sign of anyone other than Giles, who
was on the sofa, long legs stretched out in front of
him as he read one of the Sunday papers strewn
everywhere. He glanced up, getting to his feet as she
started down the stairs.

'You look better,' he commented.

She looked round, frowning. 'I thought you said
you had company.'

'I do.' He whistled, and in rushed a beautiful choc-
olate-coloured Labrador bitch, who greeted her master
with exuberant affection before turning her attentions
to his guest. Eliza gave Giles a fulminating look as
she crouched down to fondle the dog.

'Do you mean to say *this* is the lady I've tidied
myself up for?'

'The very same. Poppeia of Winterhulme, to give
her the full title, but you can call her Poppy.'

'You're a beast! But she's a beauty, Giles.' Eliza
stroked the shapely head laid so trustingly on her knee.
'Where was she last night?'

'Still in kennels after my trip.'

'Is that why you went out this morning? To collect
her?'

Giles put a hand on his heart. 'Nothing else would
have induced me to desert you on your bed of pain,
I swear.'

'Pull the other one, Giles!'

'Don't you believe me?'

'You forget I've known you a long time.'

'I forget nothing—unfortunately.'

They eyed each other in a sudden return to hostility, then abruptly Giles said, 'Eliza, I'm sorry. Perhaps it doesn't have to be like this.'

Her dark eyes narrowed in her still pallid face. 'Like what?'

His mouth twisted. '"Daggers drawn" is the popular phrase.'

She looked away, at a loss how to reply.

Giles stared broodingly at her averted face. 'Eliza,' he said after a while, 'when you were a child and I came to stay at your parents' house for the first time with Rob, how did you feel about me?'

She thought it over at some length, remembering the lanky, superior youth who'd seemed so god-like to the ten-year-old Eliza. 'At first I resented you a bit because Rob never had time for me when you were around. But as the years went by Gemma and I both developed violent crushes on you.'

'Teasing again?' he asked with rancour.

She coloured painfully. 'Must you use that word?'

His face set. 'I apologise. But if this crush of yours was fact, I never suspected it. Gemma was blatantly obvious, constantly trailing round after me, but you were always with your pony, or doing homework. I never had any inkling about the way *you* felt.'

'No one did.' Eliza smiled wryly. 'I was into the Brontës at the time. And there you were, about a foot taller than Rob, like a great blond Heathcliff—how I languished over you in secret! But unlike Gemma, who sails through life free of such things, I grew up with braces on my teeth, and suffered from puppy fat and spots and agonies of shyness. I took great care *not* to show my feelings—to you, or anyone else.'

Giles eyed her dourly. 'I don't remember you as an ugly duckling, but if you were you certainly turned into a swan at some stage.'

She shrugged. 'Natural progression. By the time I went to art college I'd shed the braces, the weight, the spots and my calf-love. In short, I grew up.'

'By which time I was working and had a place of my own, with no excuse to look on the Markham household as a second home any longer.' Giles's gaze locked with hers. 'I saw you often enough, of course: Christmas, special occasions and so on. But my first consciousness of you as a stunningly attractive woman was at Rob's wedding.'

Eliza made a violent gesture of repudiation, startling the dog. 'I don't want to discuss that again——'

'It's better we do,' he said forcefully, silencing her. 'I remember how surprised I was at Sally's choice of bridesmaids. She's a darling girl, and the apple of Rob's eye, but not even her mother could call her a beauty. I thought she was extraordinarily sporting to want the stunning Markham twins trailing her down the aisle.'

'It was entirely her own idea—besides, Sally was a lovely bride.'

'I hadn't seen you for some time when you came drifting towards me at the altar that day. I couldn't take my eyes off you.'

Eliza smiled scornfully. 'With Gemma alongside me?'

'I didn't notice her.'

'If you didn't, you were the only one!'

'Oh, I noticed her later on, believe me. I had no chance to tell you how breathtaking you looked, because everywhere I turned there was Gemma.'

'So I gather,' she said stonily.

His eyes narrowed. 'What do you mean?'

She thought for a moment, then shrugged. 'We're unlikely to get an opportunity like this again, so you may as well know why I behaved as I did that day.'

'It's a problem I've often tried to solve,' he said grimly. 'You deliberately set out to punish me. That was obvious enough. What beats me was why? What had I done, Eliza?'

'Don't play the innocent!' she said bitterly. 'You know very well.'

Giles leapt to his feet. 'I haven't the slightest idea what you're talking about.'

She stared up at him with accusing eyes. 'When I said Rob would object to your seduction of his sister, I didn't mean *me*. I went gunning for you to make you suffer because Gemma came to me in tears, saying you'd taken her to your room and tried to—to force her.'

CHAPTER THREE

GILES stood like a man turned to stone, his face frozen in disblief.

'I can't believe you said that,' he said, after a long, nerve-jangling silence. 'Why in hell's name would I try to force myself on Gemma?'

'She didn't say you succeeded, only that you attempted to,' said Eliza, suddenly pierced by a terrible doubt.

'And you believed her?'

She swallowed. 'I saw no reason not to. Gemma was always telling me how much you fancied her.'

'*Fancied* her!'

'All men fancy Gemma. Why should you be any exception?'

'You're at liberty to believe whom you choose, of course,' he said, in a tone which raised the hairs along Eliza's spine. 'Nevertheless, I did not force Gemma, nor attempt to, on the day of Rob's wedding, or at any other time.'

'Then why in the world would she say so?'

'How the hell should I know?' he said bitterly. 'Why does any woman do anything? Gemma's the one to ask. Not that it'll do me any good! You'll take her word, not mine.' He moved with lightning swiftness, seizing her by the elbows as his eyes glittered coldly into hers. 'But while we're on the subject, Eliza, the word "almost" doesn't apply. If it had been my intention I would have succeeded, believe me. Not that

I've ever had to resort to force. All the ladies I've known—bar one—have welcomed my lovemaking with open arms.'

Suddenly the roar of a car engine ripped through the quiet of the afternoon, rupturing the tension in the room. Giles released his grip on Eliza to dive for the window.

'Hell and damnation, it's Paul!'

Eliza stared for a split-second in horror, then raced for the stairs to the accompaniment of vociferous barking from Poppy as Giles, cursing under his breath, went to the door. He made a peremptory gesture to Eliza to get herself out of sight, and with alacrity she darted into the spare room to perch on the edge of the bed, her heart beating like a drum.

This, she decided bitterly, was the crowning touch. Hiding in a bedroom like a character in a French farce was altogether too much on top of everything else. She sat, tense, listening to the murmur of the two voices below: the deep timbre that was Giles, and the lighter, carefully preserved Cockney overtones of Paul Wright. Fists clenched, she willed Paul to leave. Please, she thought prayerfully, don't let him settle down for a long visit! But as the minutes passed by it seemed only sensible to make herself comfortable, and she slid off her shoes so she could swing her feet up on the bed, then reached for a book of Chekhov short stories from the bedside table. She was halfway through the second story when she heard voices outside in the garden at last, the growl of the Ferrari as it started up, and finally the bang of the front door as Giles entered the house.

'Sorry,' he said, coming into the room. 'Had to offer Paul a drink. Luckily he could only have one as he's on his way to Cornwall for a couple of days. Poppy almost gave the game away, whining at the foot of the stairs to get up to you.' He eyed her quizzically. 'Are you all right?'

'I am now Paul's gone!' Eliza slid off the bed, annoyed to find her knees possessed all the musculature of damp cotton-wool.

'Careful——' Giles seized her arm, then dropped it again as she recoiled. 'For God's sake, Eliza!' He controlled himself with visible effort. 'Come downstairs and I'll make you something to eat.'

'No, thank you,' she said stiffly. 'If you'll be kind enough to drive me to the nearest bus stop I'll take myself off.'

He gritted his teeth. 'Don't be stupid. You need something inside you before you travel anywhere. Besides, I haven't the faintest idea where any buses stop round here—if any do. Have something to eat, then if you insist I'll drive you home.'

'I'd rather go now!'

'You'll eat first,' he ordered.

'Oh, very well,' she said crossly. 'I'll have a sandwich or something, since you're making such a thing of it. But after that I'm leaving—even if I have to walk.'

He gave her a look which silenced her very effectively, then took himself off to the kitchen.

Eliza found she was hungry after all by the time Giles returned with scrambled eggs and toast, and, to her shame, could have eaten twice as much as she was given.

'Not very exciting,' said Giles. 'Cooking's not my forte, I'm afraid.'

'Was it Marina's?' asked Eliza sweetly.

'No need for the past tense. She's not dead. And, since you ask, cooking's not Marina's forte, either. Her talents lie in other directions,' said Giles deliberately.

Eliza ignored the last, mainly because she was curious. 'Why did you split up?'

'Why do you want to know?'

She shrugged. 'I just wondered, that's all. You were together quite a while.'

'A year. Since Rob's wedding, to be precise.'

'Oh.'

'Marina was on hand that day, you may remember, when my ego suffered so badly at your clever little hands. After my run-in with the Markham twins, Marina's pleasure in my company was balm to my soul.'

'Twins?' said Eliza sharply. 'But you said you had nothing to do with Gemma.'

'No, I didn't,' he contradicted. 'I said I didn't force her. Or try to. Or want to. But she was a constant source of annoyance to me that day, just the same.'

'In what way?'

'Ask Gemma. Perhaps she'll tell you the truth this time.'

'All right. I will.' She eyed him warily. 'Sally was hoping you'd marry Marina, I think.'

'So was Marina. Which answers your question. She gave me an ultimatum: marriage or nothing. I object to ultimatums, so I vacated the flat we shared in Oxford. I'd already bought this place previously with an eye to renovating it, so I was able to move in straight away.' Giles shrugged impatiently. 'That's enough on that subject, I think. Give me the latest on Rob instead.'

Eliza, more than willing to discuss less emotive topics, reported that her brother and his wife were very happy in New Zealand, and the senior Markhams were, at that very moment, in Auckland for a long holiday with Rob and Sally.

'My father retired on a pension comfortable enough for him to take my mother on trips they could never afford when we were children,' she explained.

'I'm glad—they deserve it. I owe a lot to your parents. Holidays at your place were the high spots of my life when I was a boy.' Giles, Eliza knew, had been brought up by a stern, irascible grandfather after the premature death of his parents. He looked bleak for a moment, then changed the subject to Eliza's career.

Eliza gave him a thumbnail sketch of her progress so far, filling him in on her course at design school, then the subsequent menial jobs in commercial design studios, her post with her present employers.

'The difficult part was getting my name known until I had a few jobs under my belt. So far, fortunately, the ones I've done have turned out pretty well.'

'Are you expensive?'

She shrugged. 'Less so than Charmian Lucas, my employer. But of course I don't have her experience. Yet.'

'I'm sure you make up for it in enthusiasm.'

'I try.'

Giles eyed her challengingly. 'And what do you do with your spare time? Is there a man in your life?'

'Of course! I'm not in Gemma's league when it comes to numbers, but I usually have some man or other in tow. The current one lectures in art history at a local polytechnic.'

Giles eyed her quizzically. 'Serious?'

'Hard to say. I haven't known him long. Besides, Lawrence has just separated from his wife. I don't think he's in any rush to commit himself again.'

'More to the point, are *you*?'

Eliza shrugged. 'I'm quite happy the way things are. Charmian lets me rent the attic flat over the business premises, Pennington's a pleasant place to live and Lawrence is on hand to socialise with now and then. My way of life suits me very well.'

'It all sounds very sensible and well-regulated.'

'That's the way I like it——' Her mouth twisted. 'Which you probably find hard to believe after last night.'

He looked down his nose in the way which never failed to irritate her. 'True. I couldn't believe my eyes when I found you up to your tricks again. You're lucky I didn't let the cat out of the bag.'

Eliza bit back an angry retort, determined to remain civil at all costs for the short time she was obliged to remain in Giles's company. 'Last night,' she went on with care, 'was the first time in years, believe it or not.'

He smiled suddenly. 'I remember Rob hopping mad with you both more than once when you were young.'

She grinned back. 'I know. We were devils at one time. When we were separated into different streams in school Gemma even wheedled me into doing a maths exam for her once. But the best was when Mother wanted photographs for our eighteenth birthday. I hated the idea, so Gem went to the photographer on her own, changed into my dress halfway through the session, and for years the portraits hung side by side in the hall at home with Mother and Dad in blissful ignorance that both were of Gemma.'

'I remember the fuss when they found out!' Giles eyed her narrowly. 'And what were you up to during the photographic session, I wonder?'

'Out with some boy Rob disapproved of, as far as I can remember.'

'I thought Gemma was the one who gave him trouble.'

Her eyes flashed. 'Neither of us was any *trouble*! Anyway, by the time Gem enrolled with a London modelling agency and I was in art college Rob had met Sally, so he left us to take care of ourselves.'

'A good thing he wasn't around last night.'

'That was a one-off, Giles! It won't happen again. Ever.'

'Can I have that in writing?' he enquired acidly. 'Just for the record, Eliza, what would you have done if I hadn't turned up?'

'I don't know.' She looked at him squarely. 'You can be very sure I'd have thought of something. When I make love with a man, Giles Randolph, it's because I want to, not to do my sister a good turn.'

Eliza could have kicked herself the moment the words were out of her mouth, her colour mounting as Giles's eyes lit with a cold, unsettling light.

'Yet you bring extraordinary enthusiasm to the task even when it's the latter,' he remarked, in a tone which made her writhe inwardly. 'Frankly, Eliza, I think you're wasted in interior decoration. After my ringside seat at your performance the day of the wedding, not to mention the one you gave last night, I'm convinced you'd have made your fortune on the stage.'

CHAPTER FOUR

GILES'S statement having killed all pretence at civility between them, Eliza demanded, and was granted, the favour of an immediate lift home to her flat in Pennington. When they arrived, after a journey completed in stony silence, she thanked Giles punctiliously, assuring him she needed no assistance to carry her suitcase up the flight of stairs to her flat.

He raised a sarcastic eyebrow. 'I doubt it. You look terrible.'

'Is it any wonder?' she said bitterly. 'Goodbye, Giles.' But to her mortification her hand was shaking too much to get the key in the lock. Giles promptly relieved her of the key, unlocked the door, then picked up her suitcase, looking bored.

'Don't be so tiresome, Eliza.'

'You needn't——' She stopped, swaying suddenly, as Giles and the trees opposite began to revolve before her eyes. He dropped the suitcase and seized her by the elbows, his fingers biting through her sweater.

'Dizzy?'

Eliza admitted reluctantly that she was, just a little, whereupon Giles swung her up in his arms and marched upstairs with her, deaf to her feeble protests until she was on her feet outside her own door. Without a word he went down to retrieve her suitcase, leaping back up the stairs with it two at a time, not even out of breath, she noted resentfully as he reached the little landing.

'I'm not sure you're fit to leave,' he said grimly as she muttered her thanks.

'I *am*,' she exploded, suddenly at the end of her tether. 'Just go away and leave me alone!'

Giles gave her a look which flayed, then went back down the stairs and out into the street without answering, slamming the door behind him so hard that the building reverberated.

Eliza woke next morning, astonished to find she'd achieved eight hours of unbroken sleep and physically felt very much better for it. But mentally she felt so depressed and tearful and at odds with life that she decided she couldn't face moping about the flat all day, day off or not, and surprised Charmian Lucas by reporting for work as soon as the shop was opened.

Assuring Charmian that Gemma was better and that her own pallor was due to nothing more alarming than a stomach upset, Eliza drew a mental veil over the rest of the weekend and banished all thoughts of Giles from her mind, grateful to get to grips with the work she was doing on a house intended as a wedding gift from a wealthy client to his daughter.

She put down the telephone with a rueful grin later after checking on the curtains for the eighteenth-century gem the bride would occupy on her return from a Venice honeymoon. 'When I asked for a word to describe what the lucky Lucinda requires, I didn't bargain for "romance". I just hope she's pleased with all this peach and baby blue.'

'Not your cup of tea?' said Charmian, who was fortyish, thin and unfailingly elegant, with sleek red hair secured, as always, with one of her collection of antique combs.

'Not all over the house, boss! I mean, what did she expect in the kitchen?'

'Probably never intends to set foot in there, darling!'

The work was welcome, but the effort to appear cheerful all day was so exhausting that Eliza was glad when it was time to climb the steep wooden stairs to her eyrie at the top of the building. Blanking out thoughts of the way she'd been carried up the day before, she pushed the door shut behind her with a sigh of relief, then lay in a hot bath for a long blissful interval, contemplating a peaceful evening with supper eaten on a tray. Not overjoyed when forced to leave her bath to answer the phone to Gemma, Eliza was in no mood for the lengthy monologue on Paul which followed.

'I rang you yesterday evening, but you weren't in,' added Gemma after a pause for breath.

'I came home rather late.'

Silence. 'Did—did Giles drive you?'

'Yes.' Eliza took in a deep breath, then asked the question which had been burning her brain since the day before. 'Gemma, I've got something to ask. And I want a truthful answer.'

Gemma gave a breathless little laugh. 'Goodness, this sounds serious!'

'It is,' said Eliza tersely. 'I want to know exactly what did happen with you and Giles at Rob's wedding, Gem. Did Giles really try to make love to you?'

There was a long silence on the line. Then Gemma sighed heavily. 'Oh, all *right*, Eliza—I knew this would happen the moment I heard Giles had crossed your path again. I hoped he'd do the decent thing and forget all about it. Too much to expect from the high and mighty Giles, of course!'

'Giles didn't mention it. I did.'

'*What*? Liza, I told you that in confidence!'

'I had my reasons. Anyway, he flatly denied it.'

'Well, he would, wouldn't he?'

'Gemma, stop it. Tell me what really happened that day—and I want the truth, please!'

Gemma gave another explosive sigh. 'Oh, very well. If you must know, nothing happened.'

Eliza tensed. 'What do you mean? Nothing?'

'What I say. Nothing. *Nada*. Sweet Fanny Adams! I always carried a bit of a torch for Giles, and he looked so gorgeous that day I just had to make a play for him. But the noble Giles wasn't having any. He just laughed at me, told me to run away and behave myself. I was so hopping mad with him I went flying to you in tears—of fury, I might add—and told you a little fairy-story out of spite.' She waited for a while. 'Are you still there, Eliza?'

Eliza let out the breath she'd been holding. 'Yes. I'm still here.'

'I mean, it isn't as if it did any harm,' said Gemma defensively.

'No harm!' Eliza hung on to her temper with effort. 'I flung a filthy accusation in Giles's face, madam! Now you tell me it was sheer fabrication. Thanks. Thanks a lot!'

'Don't be mad at me. Please! I'm very sorry, Liza,' said Gemma in a small voice.

'And so you should be. But the apology, sister dear, is owed to Giles. Not me.'

Eliza slammed the phone down, and stared despairingly into space for some time until the phone rang again to rouse her from her gloom. This time it was Lawrence, demanding her company for a trip to the cinema. It was the last thing Eliza felt like in the circumstances, and on the spur of the moment the only excuse she could think of sounded lame even to her own ears.

'I've got a lot of work I must polish off tonight,' she fibbed.

'Tell Charmian you've got a life of your own,' he complained. 'You spend the weekend with your sister and now you're working overtime. When do I get a look in? Do I make an appointment?'

In no condition to jolly him out of his mood, Eliza advised him tartly to ring her some other time, when he was feeling happier, and applied herself without enthusiasm to her supper.

After a bowl of soup she felt marginally better, but in no frame of mind to take more hassle from Lawrence when the phone rang yet again.

'If you're still in the same mood——' she began militantly.

'What mood?' said a very different voice from Lawrence's. 'I merely called to check on your health, Eliza.'

To her intense annoyance Eliza found her heart was hammering so much that she couldn't speak.

'Are you still there?' enquired Giles. 'Or has vertigo overtaken you again at the mere sound of my voice?'

'Sorry,' she said, clearing her throat. 'I thought you were someone else.'

'Your semi-detached swain, no doubt. He's annoyed with you?'

'If he is that's my business, Giles.'

'Don't fret. He'll be back again tomorrow—armed with roses if he's wise.'

'That's what you do, I take it!'

'Never fails. Anyway, how *do* you feel?'

'A bit tired. I put in a few hours' work today after all.'

'You should have taken advantage of your day off.'

'It's difficult when I live on the premises.'

'Nonsense. You looked like death when I left you last night. I almost turned back to make sure you weren't in a heap again outside your door.'

'But you decided against it.'

'Do you blame me?' He paused. 'I was in no mood for another of your snubs. And, to be brutally honest, my real reason for contacting you now is to ask whether you've spoken to Gemma.'

Eliza drew in a deep, calming breath. 'Don't worry—I didn't kid myself you were worried about something as trivial as my health. And of course I've spoken to her.'

'But did you ask the sixty-four-thousand-dollar question, Eliza?'

'Yes, I did!' She forced herself to speak civilly. 'It seems I owe you an apology.'

'You mean your beautiful twin actually admitted to a pack of lies?'

'No. Just to one.'

'It's the only one I'm interested in.' He waited for a moment. 'And while you were having this heart-to-heart,' he went on relentlessly, 'did you give her details of the revenge you took on her behalf?'

'No!' said Eliza with passion. 'It's not something I even think about, let alone discuss, Giles Randolph. I wish it had never happened. But it did happen, and for all the wrong reasons, so all I can do is apologise for subjecting you to an experience you remember with such obvious distaste.'

For the second time in an evening she slammed down the phone, but this time she sat with her head in her shaking hands, half dreading, half hoping it would ring again. When it remained obdurately silent she dragged herself off to bed and spent a long time telling herself how much better off she was now the unfinished business with Giles was well and truly settled. Now she could put the famous incident out of her mind and never think of Giles Randolph again.

As a means to this sensible end Eliza was profoundly grateful for the absorbing nature of her work during the period which followed. Her industry delighted her client as the designs for the bride's new home were put into practice, with painters and decorators working at top speed to achieve the deadline Eliza had promised. Charmian was very generous with her praise.

'I can see I shall have to look to my laurels,' she said, a couple of weeks later.

Eliza smiled. 'That's very sweet of you, but I don't think your laurels are in much danger yet, Charmian.'

Her employer looked at her searchingly. 'Nor do you need to work yourself into the ground, my child. Go off and have a proper lunch, for heaven's sake. I'll hold the fort here, and Gray's coming in this afternoon, praise be.'

Graeme Lucas, Charmian's devoted husband, was the business brain behind her success, a hard-headed accountant astute enough to ensure the firm's financial success, while leaving the artistic flair to his wife.

'Tell me to mind my own business,' said Charmian, as Eliza got up to go, 'but it seems to me I haven't heard much about Lawrence lately.'

'I went out for a meal with him last night.' Eliza sighed. 'He's being a bit trying at the moment. Thinks I work too hard, don't spend enough time with him.'

'Is he right?'

'In a way. He's been stroppy ever since my weekend away.'

'But your sister was ill. Surely he didn't resent that?'

'He hasn't met Gemma, but he's decided she's a bad influence.'

'But she's your twin, darling!' Charmian chuckled. 'In any case, doesn't he know it's pretty uphill work trying to influence you against your better judgement, Miss Markham?'

Eliza smiled demurely. 'He's learning. But Lawrence seems a bit paranoid about anyone else taking up my time these days. To be honest I was glad to get home last night. The evening ended in a bit of an argument.' Which was something of an understatement, since the root of the problem was the one which caused all her rows with Lawrence—his desire to share her bed.

Charmian nodded sympathetically. 'He's very good-looking, of course, in a moody, Byronic sort of way, but Lawrence does rather strike me as difficult.'

'I think the rejection by his wife cut deep.'

'Would you mind if she wanted him back?'

Eliza thought it over, then stared at Charmian, rather shame-faced. 'I suppose it wouldn't exactly ruin my life.'

Charmian pursed her lips. 'Are you sure you spent that weekend with Gemma? You haven't been the same since. It wasn't a naughty one somewhere with another man, by any chance?'

Eliza flushed, said something non-committal, then hurried off to lunch as bidden. When she returned, an hour later, Charmian was waiting for her with unusual impatience.

'While you were out, Eliza, a man with a very sexy voice rang to make a request for your services.'

'Really?' said Eliza, pink with gratification. 'Did Lucinda Mowbray tell him about me?'

'No idea.' Charmian consulted the appointments book. 'It's a Giles Randolph of Tithe Barn, Little Rencombe.' She looked up, eyebrows raised. 'Ah! The name not only rings a bell, but a deafening peal, I see.'

'He's an old schoolfriend of my brother's,' said Eliza with perfect truth, her colour high. 'Rob must have put in a good word for me.'

'Anyway, he can't ring back until later. I gave him your private number upstairs to arrange a meeting, since it's you he wants.' Charmian eyed Eliza with interest. 'Does he match the voice—tall, dark and handsome and all that?'

'Two out of three,' said Eliza, not mentioning that the client in question already had her telephone number. She collected a colour chart from her desk. 'I'd better get back to the lucky Lucinda. If anyone wants me I'm at the love-nest.'

When the doorbell rang later that evening, Eliza, in no mood for a visit from Lawrence, and already on edge at the prospect of a phone call from Giles, felt a rush of near panic at the sound of the latter's unmistakable tones over her intercom.

'Eliza, it's Giles. I was in the neighbourhood so I chanced finding you in. Can I come up?'

'Yes—yes, of course.' Eliza pressed the button, casting a wild eye round the flat, then down at herself in despair. Trust Giles to catch her in ancient jeans and a T-shirt.

When she opened the door to his knock Giles seemed to fill the minuscule landing. He looked brown and fit in a striped Cambridge-blue shirt and dark trousers impeccably tailored to his slim hips and endless length of legs, his suit jacket suspended by its loop over his shoulder. 'I hope I haven't come at an inconvenient time,' he enquired, raising an eyebrow.

'No—not at all.' Eliza waved him into the sitting-room, trying not to think of the last conversation they'd had together.

'It struck me you could have been entertaining a lover.'

'Not tonight.'

They regarded each other in wary silence for a moment, then Eliza smiled brightly, waving a hand at her surroundings.

'Anyway, now you are here, what do you think of my little retreat, Giles?'

He took his time in examining walls rag-rolled in a subtle mixture of biscuit and pink, small dormer windows curtained from ceiling to floor with over-blown damask roses printed on beige glazed cotton. Eliza, briskly professional, told him she'd covered the sofa herself in coffee linen, had the two odd chairs upholstered in buttoned velvet a shade or two darker, and chosen the carpet because its trellis pattern incorporated all the colours in the room.

'Very inviting,' approved Giles, in the voice Charmian had found so sexy. 'This, I take it, is all your own personal taste.'

'That's right. Warts and all—which reminds me. Charmian said you rang up to engage my services today. Do you mean it? It's the last thing I expected after the things I said on the phone.'

He looked at her levelly. 'I've had a long-distance chat with Rob since then. He hinted that you could probably do with the work if I was serious about turning Tithe Barn over to a professional.'

Eliza nodded, enlightened. 'Oh, I see. I thought it couldn't have been your own idea! But in the circumstances are you sure you want me to do it?'

'Why not? My house needs doing up; you're an interior decorator. It seemed like a simple equation.' He shrugged. 'But if you don't want the job, don't worry. I'm sure I'll find someone else easily enough.'

Eliza swallowed her pride. 'I wouldn't dream of refusing. I'd have to explain why to Charmian if I did. *And* to Rob,' she added, grimacing.

'Right. That's settled, then. May I sit down?'

'Of course.'

'Will this sofa hold me?'

'Try it.' Eliza pulled herself together. 'Can I offer you a drink?'

'No, thanks. I came to visit a client in Pennington earlier on, so it seemed like a good idea to kill two birds with one stone and ask you to bury the hatchet and join me for a working dinner. I thought we could discuss my requirements over a meal somewhere.'

'I'd already started to put supper——' She paused, eyeing him uncertainly. 'You could share it, if you like.'

His eyes narrowed. 'Am I brave enough, I wonder, remembering our recent exchange of pleasantries?'

'Afraid I'll poison you?'

He gave her a wry smile. 'No. That's *not* one of the things I'm afraid of where you're concerned. But don't you have plans for this evening?'

'As it happens, no.'

'No date with your semi-detached suitor?'

'His name's Lawrence, and no, I haven't. Otherwise I'd have sped you on your way,' she assured him tartly.

They sized each other up in silence for a moment, then Giles nodded. 'In that case I'll take advantage of your offer. Thank you. I admit I'm rather hungry. No time for lunch today.'

This information decided Eliza to abandon any idea of presenting him with the salad ready prepared in her kitchen. Leaving him to help himself to a drink, she shut herself in her tiny kitchen and relieved her freezer of a casserole intended for Lawrence at some future date. She put it in the microwave to defrost, heated it to bubbling point, then sat the dish on a hotplate while she baked some potatoes in the same way.

Giles was patently impressed when a short time later they were seated at a small round table between the windows, no apparent effort on Eliza's part having produced the wine-laden beef and mushroom casserole and jacket potatoes she served with the salad intended for her own solitary supper.

'Are you a witch, by any chance?' he asked after the first relishing mouthful. 'Did you practise a little black magic in your kitchen just now?'

Eliza smiled, shaking her head. 'I admit to having the salad ready, but the other stuff came courtesy of modern technology, via the freezer and the microwave.'

'But yours was the inspired hand which put it together originally?'

'Of course.'

'Then you've answered my question. You *are* a witch!' His narrowed blue eyes met hers with a smile of such unqualified appreciation that Eliza relaxed. Hostilities, it was plain, were temporarily suspended. And Giles in social mood was a lot easier to take than Lawrence's recent sniping.

Giles needed only a little urging to polish off a second helping, and not very much more to accept a third.

'I hope I haven't devoured the entire main course intended for some future dinner party,' he said at last, sitting back with a sigh.

Eliza assured him, quite truthfully, that she often made extra things at weekends to keep for emergencies, deciding not to mention that the dinner he'd just eaten had originally been intended for another man.

'Shall I help wash up?' he asked as she took their plates.

'No fear!' Eliza sent a wry look in his direction. 'My kitchen barely has room for me. You just sit there and I'll fetch some cheese. No pudding, I'm afraid.'

'Your magic wand doesn't stretch to puddings?'

'I make sure it doesn't.' She sighed regretfully. 'If I ate sweet things regularly *I* wouldn't be able to get into my kitchen either.'

Giles's eyes ran over her back view with pleasure as she left the room. 'I find that hard to believe,' he called.

'Why, thank you, kind sir!' She bobbed him an ironic curtsy as she reappeared with a bowl of fruit and a cheeseboard. 'I intend to stay that way if I possibly can, too.'

'Surely you didn't take my remarks about fragility and lettuce leaves to heart, Eliza?'

'Of course not. Actually, I'd forgotten them.' She braced herself. 'I only wish I could forget other things so easily.' Her eyes met his without evasion. 'There's no point in beating about the bush. I'm glad you're here tonight, Giles. I'd never have had the face to come and see you in person, and it just didn't seem the sort of thing to discuss over the phone. You've given me the opportunity to apologise properly for what I did to you that day. I should have the night you rang, but I'd only just found out that Gemma lied. The discovery was too new and raw. But I shouldn't have taken it out on you, and I'm sorry. You must be fed up to the back teeth with the Markham twins.'

'A delightful pair—but, like Byron, dangerous to know,' he agreed broodingly. 'But let's get one thing straight, Eliza. After you left me flat the day of the wedding I felt like murdering you, I was so frustrated—and bloody well hurt that you could do such a thing to me, too—but distaste had nothing to do with it.' His eyes held hers. 'Until you brought things to such a dramatic halt, it was the most erotically exciting encounter I'd ever experienced with a woman.'

Eliza blushed to the roots of her hair. 'Please, Giles——'

'No,' he interrupted. 'Let's get it all out in the open. What I do blame you for is the fact that it stampeded me straight into an affair with Marina Foster.'

'Hey, steady on! What's that got to do with me?'

'Everything. Rejection from a woman was a new experience for me. That it was meted out by someone I'd always been so fond of made it twice as hard to take. And there was Marina, behaving as though I was the answer to her every prayer. Quite unwittingly she provided much needed balm for my wounds. And in no time we were living together, with everyone expecting us to be next down the aisle.'

'Why weren't you?'

Giles stared at her sombrely. 'Because marriage is an institution which lacks appeal for me. With anyone. I was happy enough with things the way they were, if I'm honest. If Marina had agreed to keep to the status quo I'd still be living with her in Oxford, I'd be selling Tithe Barn on to someone else——'

'And you'd never have met me again,' she finished for him.

'Yes,' he repeated without inflexion. 'I'd never have met you again.' His eyes narrowed. 'I'm curious. Tell me, Eliza, if revenge hadn't been your motive that day, would you have run away as you did?'

'No,' she said promptly. 'Because I wouldn't have been there in the first place.'

He smiled sardonically. 'Such soul-destroying honesty, Eliza. Though I prefer it to the hostility you bristled with before. I contemplated waving a white flag when I arrived.' He took an apple and began to peel it neatly.

Eliza watched him thoughtfully. 'Giles.'

He looked up. 'Yes?'

'Talking of white flags——' She hesitated.

'Go on.'

'What would you say to a state of truce?' she said in a rush. 'I mean, if you're serious about wanting me to do your house it would make things so much easier. It's vital in my line of work to be on good terms with the client.'

He gazed at her in silence for so long she had trouble in sitting still. 'If that's what you want, Eliza,' he said slowly at last. 'Truce it is. Shall we drink on it?'

She smiled brilliantly in relief. 'Why not? Brandy?'

'Just a thimbleful,' he said, and stretched out his long legs, to the peril of the table.

'Go and sit on the sofa,' she said hastily.

He laughed. 'Now you can see why I need a barn to live in.'

She looked at him searchingly as she handed him a glass. 'Which reminds me. One thing I want to make clear. I'll look at your place and give you my ideas and an estimate and so on, Giles, but feel free to withdraw and give the job to someone else if my proposals don't work for you. Rob or no Rob, you must be honest. Taste is a very personal thing. An experienced architect like you must have pretty firm ideas about what you want.'

'Doesn't every client?'

'Well, yes. But I usually try to steer the less informed ones away from anything totally unsuitable.' Eliza eyed him wryly. 'I can see sparks flying if my ideas clash with yours, Giles.'

He returned the look, unmoved. 'We're both professionals, Eliza. There's no reason why we shouldn't work together in reasonable harmony. You've seen the place. You must know whether you'd like to take on the job.'

Amused by a mental picture of Charmian's reaction if she refused, Eliza smiled wryly. 'Since you've taken a short-cut via my employer, I don't have much choice.'

'I suppose I've forced your hand.' He shrugged. 'But I thought if I came to you first you might say no.'

'Why on earth would I do that?'

'Hang-ups about misplaced revenge, perhaps?'

'My dear Giles,' she said with asperity, 'a job's a job. I can't afford the luxury of personal feelings. If you want me to do the work I'll do it, believe me.'

They exchanged a long, assessing look.

'All right. Deal,' said Giles briskly. 'When can you start?'

Eliza thought it over, calculating how long it would take to complete Lucinda Mowbray's house. 'Fairly soon—though I suppose,' she said consideringly, 'I could fit some of your stuff in at weekends, if you want it done in a hurry.'

'Do you usually do that?'

'If it's necessary, yes. And I shan't be doing the donkey work,' she assured him. 'There's a team for the actual painting, another for the curtains and so on. As soon as they finish on my present assignment I'll ask Charmian if I can turn them loose on you. I sometimes give a hand where necessary, but——'

'You're the brains rather than the brawn.' He reached for his jacket and took out a diary. 'When could you fit in a visit to Little Rencombe to start the ball rolling?'

'I'm tied up during the week for the time being, I'm afraid.'

'Then how do you feel about spending a Sunday at Tithe Barn? I'll give you lunch and you can look the place over.'

'This Sunday?' she asked doubtfully.

'Short notice, I suppose. No matter, the following weekend would do.'

'Whatever you prefer.'

Giles gazed at her expressionlessly. 'I *prefer* this Sunday.'

'All right.'

'Good. The sooner you start on it the better. Since your disparaging remarks about porridge I'm very conscious of the aesthetic shortcomings of Tithe Barn.'

Eliza was silent for a moment, wondering if she dared broach the subject she'd been curious about from the moment she heard Giles wanted her to decorate his house. 'Is there any rush about this?' she asked at last. 'I mean, do you have some sort of deadline?'

'No.' Giles frowned. 'Why? Is there a problem?'

'None from my point of view. It's just that clients often have something they're aiming for. My present lady is about to get married.' Eliza shrugged. 'You were very clear on your attitude to matrimony, but some lady ready to settle for less might be about to move in with you.'

He shook his head decisively. 'No. At least, not at this precise moment in time.'

'My sole reason for asking, you understand, is that where a woman's involved I like to consult her first, find out her taste and so on.'

'Of course!' He smiled sardonically. 'But don't worry, the only taste involved where Tithe Barn is concerned is mine. And yours, of course.'

She nodded briskly. 'Right. Then I'll be over on Sunday morning. Since you can't cook, would you like me to bring lunch?'

'Certainly not! I can't promise a triumph like your meal tonight, but Mrs Treasure will see I've got something edible to give you.'

'Anything will do,' she assured him. 'I shall be there to work, not socialise, Giles.'

He jumped to his feet, only narrowly avoiding collision with the overhead light. 'This is a very low ceiling!'

'Not for normal mortals, Giles.' She paused for a moment, her colour rising. 'Thank you for giving me the job.'

He shrugged. 'No thanks necessary. I'm getting expert advice, and if the terms your Charmian Lucas quoted today are anything to go by I'm not being robbed financially, either.'

'You haven't seen my presentation yet,' she warned. 'Remember I'm only a poor struggling architect!'

Eliza hooted. 'In a successful firm founded by your grandfather? Pull the other one!' She held out her hand. 'Goodnight, then, Giles.'

He looked at the hand for a moment, then took it in his, holding it fast when she tried to pull away. 'Don't worry, Eliza. I'm not about to pounce on you. For one thing, you might abandon me to my porridge décor and never darken my barn door again.'

'And for another?' she said evenly.

'To set any fears you may have at rest, I think we should discuss this rather inconvenient chemistry that exists between us—no, hold on a minute. Hear me out.' His eyes held hers implacably. 'It's pointless to pretend it doesn't exist.'

Eliza's gaze dropped. 'What are you saying, exactly?'

'That it needn't trouble you. The very fact that you could think me capable of behaving like an animal with your sister puts a very effective brake on my libido where you're concerned, Eliza.'

'Good,' she said matter-of-factly. 'Lawrence would object—strongly—if he thought I was working for someone who had designs on my body.'

He ducked his tall blond head through her doorway and stood surveying her inscrutably from the landing. 'The only answer which leaps to mind would place such a strain on our truce, Eliza, that I won't trouble to make it. Thank you for dinner—*au revoir* until Sunday.'

CHAPTER FIVE

AFTER a Saturday spent tenting Lucinda Mowbray's bedroom in miles of blue silk Eliza felt very little enthusiasm for a jazz concert in the evening, nor for the late meal Lawrence took her to afterwards. Despite the volume of sound she found herself dozing at one stage, a crime which invoked deep disapproval from her companion. The evening went from bad to worse when afterwards at supper she was so deep in thought about the truce she'd proposed to Giles, she failed to hear a very involved speech Lawrence directed at her over their tagliatelle. When he repeated it, tight-lipped, Eliza stared at him in such blank astonishment that he lost his temper completely and chivvied her out of the restaurant at such speed that they were outside in the rain before she could ask for a pudding.

'You look a trifle wan,' remarked Giles next day, when she arrived at Tithe Barn. He helped her out of the car, eyeing her dark-ringed eyes as Poppy gave the visitor a rapturous welcome. 'Problems with crustaceans again?'

Eliza stooped to hug the dog, assuring Giles that her digestive system had nothing to do with it. Pleased to find their truce seemed to be working, she relinquished the dog and would have heaved a large holdall from the back seat, but Giles forestalled her.

'Give me that,' he ordered, hefting the bag in some surprise. 'What the blazes have you got in here?'

'Just samples and colour charts and so on, and a few photographs of work I've done before. I thought it might give you an idea of my capabilities.'

'I have perfect trust in your capabilities,' he assured her smoothly. 'Now, would you like to sit in the sun behind the house for a while? I can offer you tea, coffee, wine, gin—or various fruit juices I laid in solely for your benefit.'

Eliza was grateful for the opportunity to sit in the sun for a while. Her flat was ideal in many ways for her particular requirements, but had no place to sunbathe. Giles, with Poppy in close, fussing attendance, led her through the cavernous coolness of his living area, and opened a side door on to what had once been a farmyard, and was now a lawn planted in the L-shape between the main building and the kitchen quarters. To her amusement the garden furniture consisted of two ancient steamer chairs, and a stone urn topped by a circular tray as makeshift table.

'I thought I might alienate my interior designer if I purchased something smarter without consultation,' said Giles, smiling.

'I should hope so!' Eliza fished sunglasses from her bag and sank into one of the deckchairs gratefully. 'I mustn't laze about for long, though. I came here to work.'

'What else?' he said drily, and went off to fetch their drinks.

It was very peaceful in Giles's garden. Other than continuous birdsong and the soporific hum of bees among the flowers the only intrusion on the quiet was a distant chug of some farm machine far away in the fields. Her hand fondling a gently panting Poppy

Eliza began to relax, feeling herself unwind as she turned her face up to the sun.

'Good,' approved Giles as he came back with a tray. 'You look better already.'

'I feel better.' Eliza accepted a tall, ice-filled glass of fruit juice gratefully. 'Just what I needed.'

'Bad day yesterday?' Giles poured himself a beer then stretched himself on the other chair.

'Tiring,' she admitted. 'In fact the only drawback about this peaceful scene is the heavenly blue of that sky. It reminds me of Lucinda Mowbray's bedroom ceiling.'

'I thought you weren't involved in the actual painting.'

'I'm not. I spent yesterday tenting the ceiling of the nuptial chamber in acres of blue silk.' She chuckled as Giles grimaced in distaste. 'Don't worry—it's the last thing I'd suggest for this place.'

'Bloody good thing, too.' His eyes met hers. 'Tithe Barn doesn't run to a nuptial chamber, anyway.'

'Then there's no problem,' she said lightly, looking away.

He laughed suddenly. 'It's to be hoped your client's choice of décor doesn't have a disastrous effect on her bridegroom's virility.'

'If it does, Lucinda will jolly well have to get someone else to take all that stuff down. I felt half dead by the time I finished.'

'You look half dead today, too.'

'Oh, my job isn't to blame for that. It was the social activities afterwards which did the damage.'

Giles preserved a stony silence.

Eliza turned wide, innocent eyes on him. 'Why, Giles, what *do* you think I meant?'

'Exactly what you intended me to think!' He got up to refill her glass.

Eliza drank some of the fruit juice, then set her glass down. 'Just for the record,' she said evenly, 'I went with Lawrence to a jazz concert, and on afterwards to a late supper, over which he told me his wife wants a divorce. He asked me to marry him.'

Giles gave her a searching look. 'And did you give him an answer?'

'No, not yet.' Eliza had been so abstracted by the time that she'd not only missed the news which led up to Lawrence's proposal, but the punchline as well. The result had been an acrimonious quarrel on the way home, culminating in a hostile parting, with no answer to the proposal either requested or given.

'Surely you must know what you mean to say?'

'Of course I do. I just haven't said it yet.' She finished her drink then jumped to her feet. 'Can I give you a hand to get lunch? If you don't mind, I'd like to eat early so I can get on this afternoon.'

Giles downed his beer and started up, but his chair, obviously long unused to supporting anyone, let alone someone of Giles's stature, gave off a hideous creaking noise and collapsed under him, leaving Giles sprawled on his back.

'*Giles*! Are you hurt?' Eliza dropped to her knees beside him, panicking for a moment as he lay like a statue, eyes closed. She leant over him, touching an unsteady hand to his cheek, then gave a smothered gasp as Giles's arms shot up and pulled her down on top of him, one hand bringing her head down for the kiss she was helpless to avoid. She gave a protesting murmur which he stifled with the ruthless skill of his mouth, her body suddenly boneless as she yielded to arms which drew her down to him. Then sanity returned with a rush, and with it came fury for herself for letting him trick her.

'*Bastard*!' she panted, struggling to free herself from arms which held her like iron bars. She glared, panting, into the molten blue eyes below her own. 'That was a low-down, rotten trick to play.'

Giles wasn't even listening. His arms tightened as he rolled over to imprison her beneath him on the cool grass, taking advantage of her outraged gasp to invade her mouth with a caressing tongue as he kissed her deeply again, at which point Poppy decided this was a game everyone could play, licking both faces in turn, and Eliza scrambled up ungracefully, face flaming as she shook off the helping hand Giles leapt to his feet to offer.

He shrugged, unrepentant. 'The fall was an accident.'

'But not the rest of it!' She glared at him. 'You *said* my opinion of you put a damper on—on that kind of thing.'

'I should have said barring accidents, apparently.' He winced as he gingerly probed his scalp beneath the thick gold hair.

Eliza's eyes softened. '*Did* you hurt yourself, Giles?'

'I assure you I didn't run the risk of concussion just to lure you into my embrace,' he said caustically.

'So I take it that kind of thing won't happen again?'

'Oh, for God's sake, Eliza—it was only a kiss,' he said wearily. 'Let's forget it and have lunch.'

From then on Giles preserved a carefully neutral manner which Eliza took as an effort to convince her that the truce might still, after all, be a feasible proposition. Once she'd put the incident behind her she began to enjoy her day. The meal was long and leisurely, despite her determination to get to grips with her job. But afterwards Giles provided expert help as she measured rooms and drew up a survey, and listened with gratifying attention when she gave him her suggestions for a furniture layout.

As expected, Giles had clear-cut ideas of his own, particularly for the dining-room, where light and warmth were needed for the relatively small north-facing room.

'Agreed,' said Eliza. 'I'd suggest cotton in wide stripes of coral and cream for the walls and chair seats. Keep the existing curtains, but with heavy silk ropes to tie them back, and I fancy an ox-blood tint for the woodwork.' She turned to him, eyes bright with enthusiasm. 'But to show up the rafters in the main living room you could keep the walls paleish, if you like, perhaps rag-roll them like mine with a warmer colour mixed in, and a deeper, toning colour for the paintwork. A warm tawny shade like your chair for the curtains——'

'Velvet?'

'No. Heavy raw silk, perhaps with a pleated edge in apricot-yellow for accent. I'll look for rugs with rust-reds and ochres to warm up this carpet—which is much too good to throw out, unfortunately——'

'Fortunately from my point of view,' he said drily.

Eliza halted. 'Just stop me if you don't like anything. Of course I'll work it all out with a proper colour board and samples, and a price list. If you can run to it I think a jacquard-patterned sofa in dull gold would live in harmony with all this butch leather of yours, and that little round table with the battered top would look wonderful covered with a velvet cloth, perhaps with a dramatic silk bobble fringe, and a framed photograph or two sitting on it—am I boring you?' she said suddenly. 'I do rather tend to get carried away.'

'No. You're not boring me.' The eyes trained on her face told her nothing. 'Even as an argumentative child you were never boring. Besides, it's obvious you love your work. Am I right in thinking you see the finished result in your mind's eye—like a photograph?'

'Exactly!' She smiled at him in pleased surprise. 'How perceptive of you, Giles. I think you'll be pleased with my scheme.'

'I'd better be. None of it sounds very cheap!'

'Buy cheap, buy twice!' She eyed him expectantly. 'How about the bedrooms?'

His bedrooms, he said firmly, could wait until a later date. 'My name's not Croesus, lady!'

'Oh, all right,' she said, crestfallen. 'But at least splash out on a water-colour or two for the spare bedroom.'

Giles, it seemed, had various works of art still in their crates, and promised to give her a free hand as to their disposal. 'But not today! A swift look at the kitchen, a spot of ball-throwing for Poppy, then I'll make you some of the tea you're so addicted to.'

The kitchen was large and cavernous, the only fittings, apart from a cooker and refrigerator, a Georgian dresser and the original stone sink complete with green-crusted brass taps. After showing Giles pictures of mammoth white-enamelled double sinks as the nearest modern substitute, Eliza suggested they set one into the tiled top surface of a row of cupboards made of wood as close as possible to that of the dresser, which had been painstakingly restored by a local craftsman Giles had discovered, via his Mrs Treasure.

'Primrose walls and deeper gold paintwork, cupboard tops tiled in a mixture of greens shading from lime to jade,' said Eliza, darting from one side of the room to the other. 'Plain leaf green curtains and striped blinds, ochre and white, I think. You approve?'

'Anything you like other than those frilly things.'

'Knicker-blinds, Charmian calls them.'

Giles grimaced, then held open the door imperatively. 'Right. That's enough for today, Eliza.'

After tea Eliza promised to present her scheme formally to Giles by the end of the week, then took her leave. 'Thank you for my lunch,' she added, as he stowed her grip in the back of her car.

'Thank you for coming—even more for staying,' he added drily. 'At one point I thought I might have lost the services of a very talented designer.'

'It was touch and go,' she agreed, her smile crooked. 'No more chemistry lessons, please.' She yawned suddenly. 'Sorry, Giles. I must have an early night. I'm tackling Lucinda Mowbray's drawing-room tomorrow, a task requiring not only health and strength, but also my not noticeably large stock of patience. The bride insists on coming along to give me a hand, heaven help me.'

Giles leaned an elbow on the car roof, eyeing her. 'Talking of brides, what answer will you give *your* suitor?'

'I can't tell you that, Giles. It's only fair to let Lawrence know first.' Eliza smiled up at him serenely.

'I'll keep you up to date when I present my finished scheme for your approval.'

'Could you have it ready by Friday?'

'I should think so.'

'I'm due to see my Pennington client again in the afternoon,' he said casually. 'If you're free that evening we could discuss your scheme over dinner perhaps. My treat this time.'

Eliza considered the idea for a moment. If she turned down Lawrence's proposal, as she intended, she was likely to be free most evenings from now on. And it wouldn't be the first time she'd had a meal with a client, though never with one as large and male and attractive as Giles Randolph.

She nodded briskly. 'Then thank you. I'll do my best to have everything ready by Friday.' She gave Poppy a last pat and got in the car. 'Goodbye, Giles.'

'*Au revoir*, Eliza—drive safely.'

Most of Eliza's time the following week was spent in a hectic supervisory round of curtain-hanging, carpet-laying, and meticulous arrangement of expensive antique furniture in the future home of Lucinda Mowbray, who, with the wedding only a few days away, was in such a state of excitement that she was a great deal more hindrance than help on the days she insisted on putting in an appearance for a minute or two.

To add to Eliza's fatigue, Lawrence, flabbergasted at having his proposal turned down, lay in waiting each evening when she finished work, declaring he'd keep on asking her to marry him until she gave in and said yes.

'He's driving me mad, Gem,' she said to her twin, who was very conciliatory these days during their telephone conversations. 'He wasn't nearly so attentive when he thought I was his for the asking.'

'Tell him to get lost,' advised her sister, then asked diffidently after Giles. 'How was he when you made your apologies, Liza? Did he say vile things about me?'

'Not many. I came in for all the flak.'

'Why, for heaven's sake? I was the one who told the lies!'

'Ah, but I was the one who believed them.'

'Oh, Liza, what can I say? Would it do any good if I rang Giles up and grovelled? Asked him not to tell Rob?' Gemma shuddered audibly at the thought.

'Leave it. He won't do that,' said Eliza with conviction, then went on to inform her astonished sister that, after a nudge from Rob, Giles Randolph had commissioned her to do over Tithe Barn.

'Glory, Liza, that's a surprise! Does this mean you and Giles are friends again?'

'Not exactly. We've agreed on a sort of truce.' Eliza gave a wry laugh. 'It doesn't do to be at odds with a client. Bad for business. Anyway, what are you up to tonight?'

Gemma, it seemed, was making herself beautiful for a special dinner Paul had arranged that night to celebrate their anniversary.

'What anniversary?'

'It's two months since we first met, of course!'

'Oh, of course—silly me!'

'It's not funny!' said Gemma hotly, then sighed. 'I do so wish he'd propose, Liza.'

'I'm sure he will. When do I get to meet him? Officially, I mean!'

'Not yet. Can't frighten him off by trotting out my relatives at this stage.'

Since Gemma to date had flitted from one man to another without any of the fuss she was making about Paul Wright, Eliza felt uneasy when the phone call was over, and hoped that the man's intentions lived up to expectations, otherwise her sister seemed headed for heartbreak. And, whatever transgressions Gemma committed, Eliza knew she'd always feel her twin's unhappiness like her own.

Eliza was obliged to work in the evenings on her presentation for Giles, unable to spare time from her other tasks during the day. When he rang on the Thursday to confirm their dinner date Eliza felt an unexpected twinge of pleasure as he went on to question her about her response to Lawrence Shaw's proposal.

'He just won't take no for an answer, Giles,' she said with complete truth.

'Did you turn him down?'

'Yes. But he lies in wait every night when I finish work, determined to change my mind.'

'Will he succeed?'

'Who knows?'

'You should have turned him down harder,' he commented shortly. 'Tell him to take his medicine like a man and leave you alone, Eliza. I'll tell him for you, if you like.'

'Certainly not. I'm perfectly capable of coping with male attentions myself, thank you, wanted or unwanted.'

'Not always.'

'If you mean Paul Wright, that was different. I was obliged to keep him on the boil for Gemma, remember. And I succeeded, apparently.' She mentioned the anniversary celebration. 'I worry about her, Giles. She's in such a state about the man, it keeps her awake at night.'

'Hard to believe she's your twin!'

'Why?' she said indignantly. 'I'm as capable of emotion and feelings as anyone. I just take care not to let them get out of hand.'

'Haven't you ever lost sleep over a man, Eliza?'

'No,' she lied shamelessly. 'Not that I can remember.'

'You'd remember only too well if you had,' he informed her drily. 'See you tomorrow, Eliza. Don't work too hard.'

Eliza dined with the Lucases later that evening to celebrate the completion of work on Lucinda Mowbray's house, and gratefully accepted the offer of a bed for the night afterwards rather than run the risk of finding Lawrence camped out on her doorstep. These days she found it increasingly hard to believe she'd contemplated any kind of lasting relationship with him.

That her change of heart coincided with running into Giles Randolph again, she knew perfectly well. Renewing her acquaintance with a man of his calibre had opened her eyes to a certain lack in Lawrence's make-up. Until recently the latter's intellect and looks, and a certain romantic intensity about him, had blinded her to his complete lack of humour. Now she knew beyond all doubt that even if Lawrence took up residence on her doorstep permanently she'd never change her answer to his proposal.

To Eliza's relief Lawrence failed to put in an appearance as usual when she went upstairs to her flat the next evening. Message received at last, she thought, and sang in her bath as she got ready for her evening with Giles. Later, as she did her hair and face, she found that her festive mood extended to her looks. Unlike Gemma, who never looked anything other than perfect, Eliza was resigned to days when she looked no more than passable, as if her inner light was subject to fluctuation. But not tonight. Her hair shone, the burnt orange shade of last year's dress was flattering, and her face glowed with... She frowned at her reflection, jolted by the sudden realisation that the prospect of an evening with Giles had more than a little to do with her extra candle-power.

In the few minutes left before Giles's arrival she gave herself a trenchant little lecture about the dangers of laying herself open to more heartache on his account, but her heart remained obstinately light as she made sure her colour boards and samples were in order, then set out two glasses and checked that the half-bottle of Dom Perignon was chilled to the required temperature. When the buzzer sounded on her intercom she called a response to Giles's deep-toned greeting and pressed the release button.

Eliza threw open her door with a smile then stared, aghast at the sight of Lawrence at Giles's elbow, outrage on his face as Giles, before she realised his intention, swept her into his arms and kissed her at length, in a manner designed to show Lawrence he was accustomed to the privilege.

'Hello, darling,' Giles breathed, smiling into her dazed eyes. 'You look ravishing!' He kept a possessive arm round her waist as he turned to Lawrence, all smiling affability. 'Your friend and I arrived on your doorstep simultaneously, Eliza. Won't you introduce us?'

Eliza did so mechanically, conscious of the contrast between the two men. Giles, his hair streaked with gold by the sun, his face very brown, wore a custom-made grey suit of tremendous elegance. Lawrence, in one of the striped blazers he affected socially, with a spotted silk bow at the collar of his white muslin shirt, his silver-grey linen trousers the exact shade of his narrow Italian shoes, looked pale with suppressed hostility as he forced himself to shake the long, slim hand extended to him with such forceful joviality.

'I tried to contact you last night, Eliza,' he said, dawning suspicion in his eyes as he noticed the champagne.

'I was out.' She detached herself belatedly from Giles's grasp. 'Won't you have a drink, Lawrence? I'll fetch another glass.'

'Yes, do have a spot of bubbly, old chap,' said Giles heartily. 'The more the merrier for our little celebration, darling, what?'

'No! No, thanks,' choked Lawrence. 'You're obviously going out. I'll see you another time, Eliza.'

She smiled at him, trying to hide her relief as she waved him down the stairs. 'Goodnight, Lawrence.'

'I'll be back!' he assured her darkly.

Eliza felt Giles move close behind her.

'Any time, old chap,' he told Lawrence, smiling with exaggerated *bonhomie*. Eliza blew out her cheeks in relief as Giles shut the door with unnecessary force. 'Sorry about that. I should have known he'd turn up again tonight.'

Giles's geniality dropped from him like a cloak. 'I should have sorted him out good and proper, Eliza.'

'You mean you didn't?' She raised a satirical eyebrow.

He shrugged. 'You said the man had been bothering you. What better way to tell him he was on a losing wicket?'

'I think he got the message!' Eliza sighed impatiently. 'Oh, do stop looming over me so disapprovingly, Giles. I'm in the mood to celebrate. Don't spoil it.'

His eyes softened. 'All right, I won't. But what exactly are we celebrating? For a moment there, when I saw the champagne and His Nibs done up like a dog's dinner, I thought you'd given in and said yes.'

'Ah, I see. You kissed me by way of congratulation!'

'Not at all.' He smiled, the long blue eyes slitted disturbingly. 'I kissed you because I wanted to.'

'Well don't make a habit of it,' she advised him tartly, and handed him the Dom Perignon. 'Would you open this, please? I've lifted my ban on champagne so we can celebrate the completion of my work on Lucinda's love-nest. The lady's ecstatic, her papa's pleased with me because his baby's pleased, and Charmian's in receipt of a nice fat cheque.'

Giles removed the cork skilfully, allowing only the merest wisp of smoke to mark its departure from the bottle. He filled their glasses, then raised his own in toast. 'To a very clever designing lady.'

'Thank you.'

After draining her glass Eliza giggled suddenly. 'You really were dreadful, Giles—the complete hooray Henry!'

He laughed. 'The man seemed impressed.'

'Oppressed, you mean. Poor Lawrence.'

'Poor, my eye!' he snorted. 'If he's too much of a prat to take no for an answer——'

'Why are you so certain my answer's still no?'

'Because if it were yes, surely yours truly would have been shown the door, not your palely loitering swain!'

She nodded matter-of-factly. 'True. But he's not that bad, Giles.'

'Obviously not. Otherwise your relationship with him would never have progressed as far as a proposal.' Giles paused. 'Incidentally, where were you later on last night? I rang you again to say I might be held up tonight.'

'I didn't come home last night.'

His face tightened. 'Am I allowed to ask where you were?'

'Certainly not. It's no business of yours, Giles.'

'With your parents and Rob on the other side of the world, and Gemma wrapped up in her own affairs as usual, I happen to feel obliged to keep an eye on you,' he said brusquely.

'I absolve you of any obligations where I'm concerned here and now! I'm a grown woman these days, not a ten-year-old with a pony.' Her eyes flashed. 'Besides, you've known Gemma just as long. Why aren't you keeping an eye on her, too?'

'Propinquity,' he said silkily. 'I can't be in two places at once. Since my move to Little Rencombe, you're the nearest.'

CHAPTER SIX

RIGHT up to the time they arrived at the restaurant the truce tottered on the brink of destruction. But when she found she was being wined and dined at the most prestigious hotel in Pennington Eliza decided it was a pity to ruin such an unusual treat by a show of bad temper. And once diplomatic relations had been resumed Eliza was unsurprised to discover that not only was Giles an entertaining dinner companion and the perfect host, he possessed the enviable ability to bring waiters flocking without effort. Unlike Lawrence. And, in contrast to her evening with the latter, Eliza suffered no moments of abstraction during her evening with Giles. Which, she assured herself at regular intervals, was perfectly natural. For one thing, with a man like Giles as sparring partner she needed to keep her wits about her, and for another their respective careers gave them a great deal in common. And as the evening wore on they found it was even possible, after a wary beginning, to indulge in reminiscence about the days when Giles had spent a large part of every school holiday with the Markhams.

'Apart from the extraordinary resemblance, you and Gemma were very different as children,' he remarked as he drove her home.

She laughed. 'Gem loved dressing up in Mother's clothes, but my sole interest in life was my pony. When

I wasn't in school I was either riding Lucky, grooming Lucky or mucking out his stable.'

'I remember. Gemma always looked like the fairy off the Christmas tree, but you were rarely visible for layers of mud.'

'Not all the time, Giles!' Eliza heaved a sigh. 'I did so love that pony. I grieved for ages after he died.'

'But you never had another one?'

'No. Dad was quite prepared to buy me one, but I felt it was sacrilege to put another pony in Lucky's place.'

'A one-pony girl.' Giles gave her a sidelong glance. 'Is that how you'll be when you find the man of your dreams? Are you a one-man girl, too, Eliza?'

'One at a time, certainly,' she said lightly.

Giles parked his car under the trees opposite the Georgian building which housed Charmian Lucas Designs. 'Not that I'm complaining, Eliza, but it strikes me that we haven't discussed your proposals for Tithe Barn yet.'

'It wasn't very practical to cart my colour boards and so on to the restaurant, so I rather took it for granted you'd come back here afterwards.' She grinned mischievously as they crossed the street. 'And, talking of proposals, you make a splendid deterrent if Lawrence still happens to be lurking somewhere.'

'So glad I have my uses! Frankly, I don't care for the idea of this idiot making your life a misery.'

'Neither do I—not that he's an idiot, by any means.' To Eliza's relief there was no one about as she unlocked the street door. 'But perhaps he'll be put off after tonight.'

'If he's not, let me know,' said Giles grimly, following her upstairs to the flat. 'I'll be only too glad to spell it out for him.'

Eliza waved him to the sofa, frowning as she switched on lamps. 'I'd rather get the message across myself. There's no point in misleading Lawrence. He's got to accept the fact that I just don't want to marry him, not—not that I've found someone else.'

'Namely me.'

'Exactly.' Eliza looked Giles straight in the eye. 'Lawrence—and who can blame him?—got entirely the wrong impression tonight.'

'I intended him to. If it's any help, by all means tell him I'm your lover—one who'll black his eye if he pesters you any more. I don't mind.'

'Well, I do,' she said angrily. 'Gem's the one with the lovers, not me.' She breathed in deeply. 'Right. Forget Lawrence, drink some coffee and talk business. It's the reason you're here, remember.'

'*One* of the reasons,' he contradicted. 'Frankly, Eliza, I'm glad you proposed this truce of ours. It's proving rather entertaining—from my point of view, at least.'

Eliza, unsure how to respond to that, went off to make coffee, and afterwards kept firmly to the scheme and layout she had ready for him, together with the cost she broached rather anxiously once he'd approved her ideas.

'Is it a bit steep, Giles? Please be frank. I could always change some of the materials——'

'No,' he said decisively. 'It's all exactly right. I wouldn't change a thing. No doubt I'll scrape the necessary pennies together.'

Much relieved, Eliza promised to make a start as soon as possible.

Giles took a bunch of keys from his pocket, detached one of them and handed it to her. 'Then you'll need this.'

Eliza eyed it with suspicion. 'Your front door?'

'Yes. Other clients must trust you with their keys, I imagine?'

'Well, yes. But I shan't be starting on your house just yet, Giles.' Her chin lifted. 'Won't someone else need the key before then?'

He shook his head, unamused. 'If it's of any interest, I'm not in the habit of handing out my keys to all and sundry. As I believe I've told you before, ladies who visit me are not encouraged to make lengthy stays, nor to come and go as they please.'

'I'm not interested in your social life, Giles!' Eliza got up and stood there, pointedly. 'Sorry to speed you on your way, but I've had a busy week. I'm in sore need of some beauty sleep.'

'You can hardly expect me to agree,' he said without inflexion. 'You must know that every man in the restaurant envied me my companion tonight.'

Colour rushed to her face. 'If that's a compliment,' she said stiffly, 'thank you, Giles.'

'It was the literal truth,' he said, exasperated. 'Why the hell do your hackles rise if I mention your looks, Eliza? Your twin laps compliments up like a cat with a saucer of cream.'

She shrugged. 'Probably because deep inside I still feel like a spotty teenager with braces on her teeth.'

He cast his eyes heavenwards. 'Give me patience! Eliza, take it from me you're a very, very attractive lady—and the most suspicious one I've ever been privileged to meet,' he added, as she eyed his out-stretched hand as though it were a lethal weapon. He let it fall to his side wearily. 'Don't worry, Eliza. I've no intention of breaking the truce.'

She felt a pang of contrition. 'Sorry.'

His mouth twisted. 'Are you?'

'Yes.' On impulse she went on tiptoe and kissed him briefly on his lean brown cheek. 'Does that convince you?'

Giles stood like a graven image, his hands clenched at his sides. 'That's not playing fair,' he said through his teeth.

She backed away, regretting her impulse. Suddenly she realised how isolated they were from all other human contact. All the buildings around housed business premises. At this time of night it was un-likely there was another human being in the entire street, other than those walking outside in the moon-light. The cosy, inviting room seemed to shrink as Giles towered over her in silence which grew and stretched until the tension was unbearable. Eliza made a little movement with her hand, unconscious pleading in her eyes, and with a muffled sound Giles caught her in his arms and kissed her hard, then let her go so suddenly that she stumbled.

'Do you expect an apology?' he asked brusquely.

She shook her head, breathing unevenly. 'No. Why should I? A goodnight kiss is small recompense for such an expensive dinner, Giles. Nothing more than most men expect, after all.'

'It's best to expect nothing where you're con-cerned,' he said coldly. 'One avoids disappointment that way.' He strode to the door, then turned, frowning. 'By the way, take my advice, Eliza. Be on your guard where Lawrence is concerned. A male animal balked of his female prey can be dangerous.'

'Are you speaking from experience?'

He gave her a long, hard look. 'If you mean the dangerous delight of our session in a hotel bedroom together, yes. When you brought me crashing from such Olympian heights I could willingly have strangled you. So do me a favour—lock your door behind me, Eliza.'

'I always do,' she assured him. 'Contrary to your belief, Giles, I'm really quite sensible.'

He looked unconvinced. 'So you keep telling me. Nevertheless, take care. Give me a ring when you're ready to start. Goodnight.' He went swiftly down the stairs, turned at the foot to raise his hand to her, then went through the street door and closed it securely behind him.

After her non-stop rush to finish Lucinda Mowbray's house Eliza took a well-earned Saturday off, slept late as a treat, then went out to shop in preparation for a visit from Gemma, who was at a loose end because Paul was away on one of his frequent business trips. When Eliza returned, laden with carrier bags, she found Gemma drinking coffee with Charmian in the shop.

'Liza!' she cried, laughing, and jumped up to hug her twin. 'I've had such a hoot of an experience. I was trying your door when this chap came up from behind and swept me into the most madly passionate embrace!'

'What! Who?' Eliza stared at her sister appalled.

'Lawrence Shaw,' said Charmian. 'He was in a bit of a state,' she warned. 'He was getting rather nasty with Gemma by the time Gray arrived to intervene.'

'Sorry about that, Gem,' said Eliza, once they were on their own in the flat.

'He was raving about some man who was here last night, but once he realised it was me and not you he took off in high dudgeon.' Gemma's eyes sparkled. 'What *have* you been up to? Who was the other man?'

Eliza busied herself with packing her shopping away. 'Giles.'

'Giles?' Gemma frowned as she draped her slender length against the kitchen door. 'What on earth was he doing here?'

Eliza shrugged. 'I told you. He's given me a commission to decorate his new house, that's all. It's purely business.'

'If you say so.'

Eliza gave her twin a long, hard look. 'After his less than happy experience at the hands of the Markham twins, what else could it be?'

Gemma flushed. 'I suppose not.' She bit her lip. 'Frankly I thought perhaps you wouldn't want to set eyes on me for a while after—well, after finding out I lied about Giles.'

'I certainly went off you for a bit,' agreed Eliza bluntly. 'But blood, as they say, is thicker than water. Besides, it doesn't matter any more. It's just coincidence that Giles is my client for a while, that's all. Once I've done his house up I probably won't see him again.'

Gemma frowned. 'It's a mystery to me why he gave you the job!'

'No mystery. Rob asked him to. Now, tell me how the romance is going.'

Paul, Gemma told her with satisfaction, was so reluctant to tear himself away that he'd asked her to accompany him on his business trip. Afraid he'd take it for granted they share a hotel room, she'd been forced to refuse, using her visit to Eliza as excuse.

'So you're still managing to hold him off?'

'Yes. I want Paul for a husband, not a lover.'

'Isn't he champing at the bit, though?' asked Eliza. 'My short but memorable experience in his company indicated he was pretty determined to share your bed.'

'He is. And he may, with the utmost pleasure, once I've got a ring on my finger,' said Gemma, with a steely gleam in her eyes that was new to Eliza.

'Wedding ring?'

'Engagement ring would do. I merely require some sign of commitment.' Gemma's tilted dark eyes slid away from the concern in the matching pair trained on her face. 'Don't look like that, Liza. I'm not really mercenary.'

'I know that.' Eliza did know, better than anyone. Gemma had been involved with wealthy men before, but had never been the least inclined to marry any one of them.

The weekend passed pleasantly, both girls glad to laze around and do very little other than talk and enjoy each other's company as they always did. Sunday proved wet enough to keep them indoors with a selection of newspapers before they enjoyed the type of lunch Gemma never ate in London. Later, towards evening, Gemma was taking a leisurely bath when the doorbell parted Eliza, groaning, from the book she was reading.

Gemma appeared in the bathroom doorway, looking like a mermaid with her wet hair dripping on her shoulders. 'If that's Lawrence, tell him to get lost.'

Eliza pushed her glasses up into her hair and crossed the room to speak cautiously into the intercom, her eyes opening wide as a confident voice with a Cockney intonation asked if Gemma were there.

'Paul Wright's the name,' he announced.

'Yes. Yes, of course. Come up.' She pressed the button then turned to Gemma in panic. 'It's Paul— for heaven's sake get dressed!'

'He said he might come if he caught an early flight,' said her twin airily. 'I didn't tell you in case you got in a tizz. It's time he met you, anyway.' She went back into the bathroom and closed the door, leaving a horrified Eliza feeling like a Christian about to face the lions.

Bracing herself, she opened the door. Paul Wright, a damp, expensive raincoat over one arm, a duty-free carrier bag suspended from the other, blinked hard, gaping openly at the sight of her.

She smiled, and held out her hand. 'How do you do? I'm Eliza.'

'Hello!' He pulled himself together and followed her into the room, dumping the carrier bag on the floor to shake her hand. Then his face split in a wide grin as Gemma emerged from the bathroom, her hair an aureole of damp curls, but otherwise a mirror image of her twin right down to the jeans and oversized men's navy jerseys both girls were wearing.

'Hello, darling.' She went into his arms with the fluid, graceful glide mastered at modelling school, holding up her face for the kiss Paul gave her with enthusiasm before holding her away slightly. He shook his head in wonder as he looked from one face to the other.

'Crikey, Gem, I know you told me but it's still a shock.' He smiled at Eliza confidently. 'Hope you don't mind my barging in like this?'

Secretly Eliza minded quite a lot, but she shook her head, still wearing her polite smile. 'Of course not. May I offer you a drink—something to eat?'

Paul grinned, brandishing the clinking carrier bag. 'I brought you a bottle or two, but for my part I'd like a strong coffee, a wash, and then perhaps you'll let me take you both out to dinner to celebrate.'

Gemma's eyes flickered. 'Celebrate?'

He winked. 'To mark the occasion. Thought you'd never let me meet any of your family. Funny thing, though, I feel I know Eliza already.'

Which was truer than he knew, thought Eliza, avoiding her sister's eye. Glad of the excuse to make herself scarce, she went off to her tiny kitchen and closed the door firmly, preferring claustrophobia to the role of gooseberry.

The evening was a wearing experience. Paul Wright spent most of it looking from Gemma to Eliza with such undisguised relish in their resemblance that Eliza found it impossible to relax.

'If it wasn't for the hair you'd be hard to tell apart,' he remarked.

'Mine's like Eliza's normally,' Gemma assured him. 'These curls are synthetic.'

'And Gem's several pounds lighter than I am,' added Eliza without thinking.

'It was the stomach upset I had after Paul's party,' said Gemma, kicking her twin under the table. 'That lobster put paid to half a stone.'

Paul nodded fervently. 'Never seen such a change! When I came back from Cornwall she looked like a different girl.'

Eliza felt the blood rush to her face and dropped her napkin so she could pick it up again, by which time Gemma had changed the subject to Paul's trip, giving him the chance to boast of its success.

Eliza felt deeply relieved when Paul finally drove off to London with Gemma, but so much on edge she gave in to impulse and rang Giles.

'This is an unexpected pleasure,' he said, surprised. 'Something wrong?'

'I need someone to talk to,' she informed him. 'And because you're the only one I *can* talk to in this instance, you're it.' She described the nerve-racking evening, and the remark which, unknown to Paul, had almost given her heart failure.

'Gem gave me such a dagger of a look it's obvious she has no intention of telling him it was me that night. He thinks *she* had the stomach upset, which explained the weight loss next time he saw her!'

Giles laughed wryly. 'You've got to hand it her, Eliza. She's determined to get her man. And part of what she said was true enough. But the infamous lobster was responsible for *your* weight loss, not Gemma's.'

Eliza looked down at herself appraisingly. 'I suppose so. Though I rather fancy my hard graft on Lucinda Mowbray's house got rid of any pounds I've shed lately.'

'None of that when it comes to my place, Eliza,' he warned. 'Take it easy—I'm in no hurry.'

'Good. By the way, we didn't discuss a starting date on Friday. Charmian's giving lectures this week and we all help with the presentation part on those. But I could start the following week if it's convenient. The painters should be free by the Wednesday, but I could make a start on the preparation myself a day or two beforehand.'

'Do you normally do that?'

'Quite often, depending on how much we have on.' She giggled. 'Graeme Lucas calls me the best stripper in the business——'

'You can't jerk my chain with that one! I'm pretty expert at paint-stripping myself.'

'Is there anything you're *not* expert at, Giles?'

'I suppose there must be, but I can't think of anything offhand!'

Eliza decided to let that one go. 'All right if I start tomorrow week, then?'

'Yes. Poppy'll be delighted.' He paused for a moment. 'I've been thinking.'

'What about?'

'It's a fair journey between Pennington and Little Rencombe each day. Now don't bite my head off, but why not stay at Tithe Barn while you're actually involved in the work?'

Eliza blinked. 'I—I don't think that's a good idea,' she said, thinking of the tension which was never far off when they were together. 'Besides, are you sure you want that? Aren't you the one who gets restive if ladies hang about too long in your bachelor sanctuary?'

'I could make an exception in your case as it's purely a business arrangement. After all, it's common sense. Subtract the daily journey and you'd get far more done.'

'I'll think about it.'

'Proving to me how sensible you are, I take it.'

'Exactly.' She put the phone down quickly, pleased at getting in the last word; something of an achievement in her dealings with Giles.

CHAPTER SEVEN

When Eliza reported for work at Tithe Barn the following week, attired in her usual working gear of cotton jumpsuit, baseball cap and trainers, she found Giles had stayed behind to greet her, Poppy bounding at his heels in welcome as the small company van came to a halt.

'I thought you'd be long gone by this time, designing a cathedral or a supermarket or something,' said Eliza, jumping out.

'It seemed only polite to provide a reception committee.' Giles whistled, a wolfish gleam in his eyes. 'I'm glad I did. It was worth it, just to see you in your working clothes.' He eyed the suitcase she handed him. 'Does this mean you've decided to stay overnight after all?'

'If convenient, yes. Of course if you've other plans——'

'Nary a one.' He smiled a little. 'I thought it best to defer all further visitors—of your sex at least—to the day when my house emerges from its porridge chrysalis into the butterfly perfection of your design.'

She scowled at his broad pin-striped back as she followed him up the stairs. 'Let's hope you don't suffer from withdrawal symptoms by the time I've finished.'

Giles ushered her into the austere guest-room with a leer. 'I can always—er—play away, so to speak, if the need becomes pressing.'

'Don't be disgusting!'

'You brought it up.'

Eliza's eyes flashed. 'Don't let me keep you. I can manage perfectly well on my own.'

He shook his head reprovingly. 'You don't change much.'

'What do you mean?'

'As a child you were always so belligerently independent, whereas Gemma accepted helping hands as nothing more than her due.'

'Gem and I look alike, and we're on the same wavelength, but otherwise we're entirely separate people,' she informed him crisply.

'Speaking as the innocent victim of at least one of her less charming idiosyncrasies, I'm glad to hear it.' He gave her the dissecting look she found so hard to bear. 'Which only makes your performance with Paul all the more masterly.'

Eliza looked at him levelly. 'I'd rather not discuss that, if you don't mind. Now, I'm sure there's something waiting for your urgent attention somewhere, Giles. I'd hate to think I'd held you up.'

'You haven't,' he assured her, and went out, closing the door behind him.

Eliza took a moment to rally the equilibrium which seemed to desert her at the drop of a hat in Giles's vicinity, then unpacked her few belongings and went downstairs, to find Giles sitting on one of the sofas, reading a newspaper, a coffee-tray on the table in front of him.

'I thought you'd have gone by now!' she said, frowning.

He gave her a quelling look. 'It is my house, Eliza. I come and go as I please. It just seemed courteous to offer you some coffee before you made a start.'

Eliza's shamed blush disappeared under the peak of her cap. 'I'm sorry,' she muttered. 'I don't know what it is about you, Giles, but you make me forget my manners sometimes.'

He shrugged. 'Whatever it is, I'll try to keep it under control for as long as it takes to drink this coffee. By the way,' he added, 'has your spurned swain made any more trouble?'

Eliza shook her head. Lawrence, she told him, had rung her to apologise for his behavior, assuring her that although she'd turned him down as a prospective husband he was very anxious to remain her friend.

'And what did you answer to that?'

'It seemed a reasonable suggestion.'

There was silence for a while.

'Did he make any reference to me?' asked Giles at last.

'As a matter of fact he did. He was—curious about my relationship with you, naturally.'

'So what did you tell him?'

'I said you were a friend of my brother's. That I'd known you since I was a child. What else?' she added dismissively.

'What else indeed?' Giles replaced the cup on the tray and got to his feet. 'I'll heave some furniture round for you before I go.'

Tempted to say she could manage perfectly well on her own, Eliza accepted his help, partly to make up for her former rudeness, and partly because she could never have rolled up the carpet and hefted the massive furniture about with such ease on her own.

'I'll be fine now,' she panted, when everything was arranged to her satisfaction.

'Good. But I want something clearly understood,' said Giles, shrugging into his jacket.

'What?'

'If you need any more strong-arm stuff, ring Mrs Treasure. Her son Bob's a hefty lad who'll be only too glad to give you a hand.'

'Oh, for heaven's sake, Giles! I do this for a living. I'm used to heaving things around.'

'You must do as you please elsewhere, of course. But not in my house.' He clicked his fingers at Poppy. 'I'll put her out in her pen for a while, or she'll give you no peace. You can let her out for a bit when you stop for lunch.'

Deciding not to mention that she never stopped for lunch, Eliza smiled politely as Giles departed, then set to work on draping his furniture in dust sheets. She was soon immersed in sanding down the paintwork in the main room, a relatively easy task since the paint had been applied only months before. By noon, after working non-stop, she was ready to meet the far greater challenge of the kitchen, and was about to make a cup of coffee before taking the plunge when someone tapped on the open kitchen door.

'Good afternoon, miss.' A small woman, wiry and neat in a flowered print dress and hand-knitted cardigan, gave Eliza a shy smile as she deposited a large basket on the kitchen table. 'My name's Treasure. I clean for Mr Randolph.'

'Why, how nice to meet you. I'm Eliza Markham.' Eliza returned the smile warmly.

'I didn't think you'd be doing the actual work,' said Mrs Treasure, eyeing Eliza's overalls.

'I'm just doing a bit of the preparation. The professional painters can't start until Wednesday, so I'm

cleaning down the paintwork to hurry the job up.'
Eliza washed her hands under the kitchen tap. 'I'm
making coffee. Do have some with me.'

'I won't say no.' Mrs Treasure began unpacking the
basket briskly. 'I've brought your lunch, miss.'

Eliza's jaw dropped. 'My lunch——?'

'Mr Randolph says you've got to eat properly, and
I'm to see you do.' The woman smiled apologetically.
'He's a very forceful gentleman.'

'I know,' said Eliza with feeling. 'Oh, well, to be
honest now I've stopped for a minute I do feel rather
hungry.'

Expecting a packet of sandwiches, Eliza was deeply
impressed by the egg mayonnaise and crisp green salad
Mrs Treasure produced, with the added treat of home-
baked bread to eat with it.

'I hope it's the sort of thing you fancy, miss,' she
said, busily transferring various dishes from the vast
basket to the refrigerator. 'Eggs from my own hens,
and my Bob brings me special oil from the supermarket to make the mayonnaise. Mr Randolph's very
partial to it.'

'I'm not surprised!' said Eliza, mouth full. 'It's
quite wonderful.'

Mrs Treasure looked pleased. 'I mustn't be long.
My Bob'll be home soon. He only works mornings
in the supermarket. So if you want anything shifted,
just give me a shout and he'll come. Mr Randolph
don't want you straining yourself.'

'No,' agreed Eliza drily. 'He gave me his orders
before he went.'

The little woman nodded in approval, informing
Eliza that she'd brought a nice cold roast fowl for

their dinner, a few potatoes, a dozen fresh eggs and a pudding. 'I hope that'll suit you, miss.'

Eliza, inelegantly mopping up the last of the mayonnaise with a piece of bread, nodded with enthusiasm. 'Perfectly, Mrs Treasure—only do call me Eliza.'

The other woman looked diffident.

'Please?'

'Well, if you're sure,' said Mrs Treasure, and beamed as she sat down to drink her coffee. 'My name's Phyllis.'

Giles rang during the afternoon to check on Eliza's progress, informing her he'd be late home as he was making a detour to Combe Farm, the house he'd redesigned for Paul Wright.

After reporting tartly that she'd obeyed orders and eaten lunch as bidden, Eliza plunged back into her preparations on the kitchen, feeling rather like Hercules faced with the Augean stables by late afternoon, since for all her back-breaking efforts there was very little to show for her labours. By six every muscle was aching, her throat was dry and she felt thoroughly scruffy and unappetising. She had a quick romp in the garden with Poppy, then gave the dog her dinner and went off to have a bath. If she was confident she looked good it might help her to maintain an atmosphere of impersonal civility all evening. Because Giles must be left in no doubt that her sole motivation for staying the night was merely a desire to complete the work on Tithe Barn at top speed.

Hair shining and face glowing, dressed in white linen trousers and a scarlet shirt, she went downstairs to find Poppy still on her own and no sign of Giles.

Late obviously meant late. She wiped down the kitchen table, then took the admirable Phyllis's offerings from the fridge. The chicken was fragrant with herb stuffing, the vegetables were ready-scrubbed new potatoes, and alongside them sat the most luscious, tempting bread and butter pudding Eliza had ever beheld.

Eliza laid the table in the as yet unpillaged dining-room, put the potatoes on to cook, and after discovering a pot of Phyllis's mayonnaise made a green salad as an excuse to use it. By the time Giles finally put in an appearance there was nothing more to do.

'Dinner's ready, get a move on,' she said, her voice gruff to hide her sudden ludicrous shyness at the hint of intimacy in the situation.

His eyebrows rose. 'With service like this, no wonder Charmian Lucas Designs is successful.' He bent to return Poppy's enthusiastic greeting. 'Hello, my lovely girl. Have you had *your* dinner?'

'Of course she has. But I haven't had mine and I'm ravenous.' Eliza chivvied him towards the stairs. 'So hurry up with your ablutions, please, Mr Randolph, or the chicken will get warm.'

Giles went upstairs two at a time. 'Do you provide dinner for your other clients too, Eliza?' he called over his shoulder.

'Certainly not. Nor did I provide this one. Everything comes compliments of Phyllis.'

He paused on the landing, his face blank. 'Who the devil's Phyllis?'

'Mrs Treasure, of course.' Eliza brandished a corkscrew at him. 'Get a *move* on, Giles!'

Her fleeting awkwardness well under control by the time Giles returned, Eliza listened with intense interest as he gave her an account of his meeting with Paul Wright at Combe Farm. And while they kept to matters of professional interest the conversation, to her surprise, never flagged once during the simple, delicious meal.

'That was wonderful,' sighed Eliza at last, laying down her spoon.

Giles refilled their glasses, his eyes bright with sudden, unsettling mockery.

'Why the funny look?'

'It just struck me that we make a perfect picture of domesticity, Eliza.'

'Appearances can be deceptive.'

'How true,' he said without inflexion.

There was silence for a moment, then Giles smiled faintly. 'And there's a snag. Now we've eaten dinner there's nowhere to sit unless we stay here.'

'I know.' Eliza stifled a yawn rather elaborately. 'Not that I'm sitting anywhere for long. I'm sleepy. All that food on top of my labours has wiped me out.'

Irony glinted in the dark blue eyes. 'I'm afraid I stowed the television and my stereo system away in my bedroom last night. But if you fancy some music, or a look at the news, you could sit on my bed. I promise to keep to the floor,' he added softly.

She shook her head, refusing to rise. 'If I even look at a bed I'll fall asleep, Giles. Let's just stay here. Perhaps you'd be a sport and make the coffee.'

'What you really mean is that you've no intention of setting foot in my bedroom.'

'Not unless you want my professional opinion on redecorating it, no,' she said shortly.

'Pity.' Giles leaned his chin on his hands, his eyes locked with hers. 'Not that you need worry—or lock your door tonight. Truce we agreed on and truce I'll keep to. But in one way you should feel very flattered, Eliza.' He waved a hand at the table. 'Since my narrow escape from Marina's matrimonial toils, the merest hint of such unbridled domesticity from anyone else would have me rushing for the nearest exit.'

She smiled, unruffled. 'Ditto, Giles, so no problem. You're perfectly safe with me.'

He gave a bark of mirthless laughter. 'I *used* to feel safe with you. But on a certain day just over a year ago all that changed within the space of half an hour. Nowadays your company, delight though it be, smacks of danger.'

She gave him a long, hard look. 'You're in no danger from me, Giles, I promise you!'

His mouth twisted. 'You still don't get it. The danger lies with *my* baser impulses, not yours.'

Eliza's patience suddenly deserted her. 'So what? Speaking from a purely theoretical point of view, would it be so earth-shattering if two consenting adults did succumb to this chemistry you talk about?' She smiled scornfully. 'But that isn't really the problem, is it, Giles? Your baser impulses are on a losing wicket because your ego just can't cope with the fact that I believed Gemma instead of trusting you.'

Giles refilled her glass. 'For a while that was true. I wanted to wring your neck—and Gemma's—when you first told me. But the danger I'm referring to is something rather different.'

Eliza frowned. 'I don't understand.'

'It's quite simple. My basic problem is the fact that I want you, Eliza,' he said quietly, the look in his eyes leaving her in no doubt that he meant what he said even as his words took her breath away.

'Is that why you asked me to stay tonight?' Her eyes flashed coldly as she clenched her trembling hands. 'Sorry—not one of the services included in my fee.'

He sighed wearily. 'I'm still not getting through to you. Eliza, I've wanted you ever since the day I had you underneath me on that hotel bed with your hair falling down and your mouth opening to mine——'

'Stop it!' she cried in outrage, and set her empty glass down so fiercely that it cracked and overturned. 'Oh, lord, now look what I've done——'

'What the hell does it matter?' he said roughly, and reached across the table to take her hand. 'But don't worry, Eliza. Want, as my grandfather used to say, must be my master, so you're quite safe.' His grip tightened until she thought her bones would crack, then he released her hand and sat back, a bleak twist to his mouth. 'With any other woman the problem wouldn't exist. I'd have you in my bed right this minute. But because you are your parents' daughter, not to mention Rob's sister, that's not possible. If you embarked on a love affair with me your family, naturally enough, would expect marriage as a natural progression. But I'm not in the market for matrimony, Eliza—not even with you.'

'Oh, I *see*,' she said, enlightened. 'That's what this is all about. You're scared witless I'd demand a wedding ring in return for a night of blazing passion!'

'No, I'm bloody well not! But I owe too much to your parents to hurt them. And as you once said, Eliza, Rob wouldn't be over the moon if he thought I'd seduced his sister, either.'

'Oh, for heaven's sake.' Eliza got up, throwing down her napkin like a gauntlet. 'What a lot of fuss about nothing! But don't worry, Giles. Once this job is over we needn't see each other again.' She glared at the overturned glass. 'I just wish I hadn't drunk the wine. I could have driven home right now and let your precious baser impulses get a good night's sleep.'

Giles leapt to his feet and stalked round the table. 'Just go to bed, Eliza. Now, please. There's a key in the spare room door. Use it if you're scared.'

She stood her ground, glaring at him. 'Don't think I won't! I must have been mad to decide to stay, but at least it means I can start work as soon as you leave and get the job done at top speed. The faster I'm out of here, the better.' She turned on her heel and ran for the stairs, mounting them at a dangerous rate. She slammed the spare room door behind her, then turned the key in the lock with a click designed to carry to the man who'd stood like a statue, watching her retreat.

Next morning Giles took the hint and left for work very early. Eliza watched the car out of sight from the spare room window, then ran downstairs and worked non-stop through the day, driving herself relentlessly in her effort to leave everything in readiness for the professionals. Dizzy from lack of food followed by a long drive on top of a wildly busy day, she was barely through the door of her flat when the telephone rang. But instead of Giles, as she half expected, it was Gemma, in a high state of excitement.

'Guess what, Liza!' she bubbled.

'Paul's popped the question?'

Gemma sighed. 'No. Not yet. But he will! In the meantime he's done the next best thing.'

Eliza frowned. 'What, exactly?'

'He met Giles yesterday at the farm——'

'I know. Giles told me.'

'Anyway, Paul wants you to submit a scheme for the interior of Combe Farm now the construction work's finished! Isn't that brilliant? He was pretty impressed with your flat, so when Giles told him you were doing up Tithe Barn Paul decided to ask you to do his place, too.'

There was a pause while Eliza digested the information in dismay.

'Well?' demanded Gemma. 'Aren't you thrilled?'

'Of course,' lied Eliza, fingers crossed. 'But Gem, are you sure he's not doing this just to please you?'

'No chance. Paul's too much of a businessman for that.'

'He'll have to go through the normal channels, but, if he asks Charmian for my services, naturally I'll do it.' She hesitated. 'Only, if he's decorating it with you in mind as châtelaine, Gem, I'd like to know.'

'You're not the only one.' Gemma sighed despondently. 'Either way it doesn't matter, Liza. You get the kudos of a pretty pricey job even if it's not intended for me, and, if it is, your taste is always flawless, so I'll be happy. Ecstatically happy,' she added with another sigh. 'But I wish I knew, one way or another. I'm losing sleep over it. Which means I'll lose my looks, and then he won't want me anyway——'

'Rubbish, Gemma Markham,' said her twin sharply. 'Besides, if it's only your looks he's interested in, forget him.'

'My looks are all I've got to offer,' said Gemma simply.

Eliza spent a few wearing minutes shoring up her sister's morale, then slumped on her sofa, feeling drained, and in no frame of mind to answer the phone when it rang again, right on cue.

'I'm surprised you've got enough energy to pick up the phone,' observed Giles caustically. 'You must have worked yourself into the ground today to finish so soon. I obviously frightened you off last night.'

'I got everything done, so I came home.'

'You mean you ran away.'

'If you like. But don't worry. I made sure everything was ready for the painters before I left.'

'Of course. As long as the job is in train, what else is there to worry about?' he said with sarcasm. 'I suppose my remarks last night are to blame for the stampede?'

'After all that nonsense about danger and so on, do you wonder?' she said irritably. 'If you must know, Giles, I'm determined the famous truce will last out until the job is finished, so I took myself off rather than subject it to further strain.'

'Always the sensible Markham twin!'

Eliza's mouth drooped, unseen. 'Not always, as you know better than most. Which reminds me,' she added, determined to re-establish diplomatic relations, 'Gem's just been on the phone. Apparently Paul intends asking me to submit a scheme for Combe Farm.'

'Does he, now? And how do you feel about that?'

'I hate the very thought of it.'

'Don't look a gift horse in the mouth—a plum assignment like Combe Farm doesn't happen every day of the week, Eliza. You'd get a lot of career-boosting publicity out of it.'

'I know.' She sighed. 'If he approves my suggestions it's a wonderful opportunity, of course, but I just wish he'd leave it a while before contacting Charmian. I could do with some breathing space.'

Paul's request, however, arrived all too promptly. Charmian Lucas was jubilant as she instructed Eliza to present herself at Combe Farm the following Wednesday for a meeting with their prospective client.

Eliza, due at Tithe Barn the day before to oversee the installation of the new sink and kitchen cupboards, resigned herself to two consecutive, tiring journeys in sweltering summer heat and tried to look enthusiastic.

After hours spent supervising the installation of new fittings in the kitchen at Tithe Barn during the hottest day of the summer, Eliza was sorry she'd agreed to wait for Giles before setting off for home. By late afternoon the weather had turned stiflingly sultry. The moment the workmen left she unzipped the top half of her jumpsuit to a precarious depth for coolness, then fanned herself with her baseball cap as she embarked on a minute inspection of the tiled cupboard surfaces to check for flaws before giving the go ahead for next day's grouting work.

At the sound of approaching footsteps she tensed, trying to quell her frisson of excitement at the prospect Giles again. Pretending absorption in her task, she kept her eyes down and went on with her inspection.

'Hi!' she said cheerfully. 'You're home early tonight.'

When there was no answer she looked up enquiringly, then froze. Instead of Giles it was Paul Wright, lounging at ease in the open doorway as he looked her up and down in a way which, despite the heat, raised goose-bumps on her skin as she hurriedly yanked up her zip.

His laugh reinforced the feeling. 'If by any stretch of imagination I could visualise Gemma dressed like that I'd think I was hallucinating. How are things with you, Eliza?'

Eliza forced a smile, her colour high. 'As you can see, I'm hot and sticky, and so grubby I won't even offer to shake hands. Hello, Paul. Were you looking for Giles?'

'Yes—but I'm not complaining. This is unexpected, but a *very* great pleasure.' Paul advanced on Eliza, a predatory smile curving his wide, thin-lipped mouth. 'Pity I'm dashing back to town to meet Gemma. I could have gone over Combe Farm with you this evening, saved a day for both of us.'

'I'd have charged a fee just the same,' she informed him coolly.

'And I'd have paid. Whatever the price.' His sharp eyes held hers for a long, significant moment, then he glanced round the room in approval. 'What a transformation! You're good. Very good. This room was a museum piece before.'

'It's not finished yet.' Eliza turned away, talking rapidly to hide her uneasiness. 'The curtains and blinds are still to go up, but the worst is over. The new floor's down and they plumbed in the sinks and fitted these cupboards today. Tomorrow should see a big improvement——' She broke off, her smile incandescent with relief as Giles appeared in the doorway. She ran to him involuntarily. 'At last—look who's here.'

Giles took in the situation at a glance, put an arm round Eliza and kept it there as he greeted Paul, who, to Eliza's great relief, refused the drink he was offered.

'Can't stop. Came to tell you about the new caff I'm thinking about in Pennington,' he said, whistling as he looked at his watch. 'Didn't realise it was so late. I'll see you again, mate, OK? I'd better get on my bike—meeting Gemma at eight.' He cocked a bright eye at Eliza. 'Give her your love, shall I?'

'Please do.' Eliza smiled, feeling safe enough to detach herself from Giles's arm. 'Tell her I'll ring her tomorrow night after I've seen over your house.'

Giles went off to see Paul into his Ferrari, then strode back into the kitchen with Poppy frisking behind him. 'What the hell was all that about?' he demanded grimly. 'The atmosphere was thick enough to cut in slices when I walked in. What did Paul say— or do—to put the wind up you, Eliza?'

'Nothing. Nothing I can put my finger on, anyway.' She flushed, her eyes falling.

'You're lying!'

She rubbed a hand over her eyes. 'I'm not. I'm just being silly—embarrassed because I look such a mess, probably.'

'Rubbish! You look good enough to eat in those overalls——' His eyes narrowed in sudden comprehension at the look on her face. 'Ah, I see! It was Paul's reaction to your boiler-suited charms which set off your alarm system!'

'I suppose so,' she muttered uncomfortably. 'It's probably just the likeness to Gemma—he's not used to it yet.'

'And he's never seen her grubby and untidy and looking like a sexy plumber's mate. I'd say he was taken by the contrast, not the resemblance. It's the first I've heard about any venture in Pennington, too. What—or who—gave him that idea? I wonder.' Giles stretched mightily. 'Lord, it's hot. Have a drink before you go. Or have I forfeited the pleasure of your company altogether?'

'No, of course not.' She met his eyes very directly. 'I'll have a quick drink, but then I must go home to scrub off some of this dirt. Tomorrow morning I need to present myself at Combe Farm groomed to the eyebrows, looking like the very model of an efficient interior designer. Otherwise Paul won't give me the job.'

He gave her some fruit juice, frowning in reproof. 'Of course he will. And you take it, Eliza. Grasp it with both hands. Combe Farm's the interior designer's dream: a blank canvas waiting for you to transform it into a masterpiece, and with unlimited cash at your disposal into the bargain. Who could ask for more?' He eyed her narrowly. 'But there *is* more, obviously.'

'Yes. I just want him to propose to Gemma. She's my other half, remember, Giles. I feel her pain like my own——' She stopped, biting her lip.

'Who knows that better than I?' he said bitterly. 'I suffered the backlash from it on one memorable occasion, if you recall.'

She brushed back a lock of hair, eyeing him warily. 'I suppose you find it hard to understand the fact that I forgave Gemma so easily——'

'Somewhat. But forgiveness *is* easy when you love someone. So I've heard.'

She looked at him sharply, but Giles's face was inscrutable, giving her no clue to his thoughts. 'If Gem's happiness really does depend on Paul Wright,' she said, depressed, 'I just wish he'd get on with it and propose—as long as it's a proposal of marriage, of course!'

CHAPTER EIGHT

ELIZA made the long journey to Combe Farm to meet Paul Wright next morning, convinced after a night's sleep that she'd imagined anything out of the ordinary in his manner the day before. Today there would be no maidenly vapourings on her part. She would be efficient, businesslike and so inspired with her suggestions that Paul would soon discover she was brilliant at her job, not just Gemma's double.

Combe Farm delighted her. Originally a modest three-storey house with dormer attic windows, by Giles's design it had been given a gabled end wing to house a drawing-room and master bedroom, in preference to knocking any of the original rooms into one. As Eliza drew up in the car Paul emerged from his front door, radiating energy in skin-tight jeans and a sweatshirt printed with the name of a London gymnasium.

'Eliza, you're early. I like that.' He held out his hand, and she shook it briefly, her polite smile disguising a sharp pang of dismay. The gleam in his bright, street-wise eyes told her quite plainly there'd been no mistake on her part the night before. Eliza had enough experience of men to know that given an inch Paul would have no hesitation in taking the proverbial yard, Gemma's sister or not. Probably, in some perverse way, he was even turned on by the idea. Glad of her dark-rimmed spectacles and primmest tailored suit for armour, she returned his greeting briskly, produced a notebook and suggested they get on as quickly as possible.

But Eliza forgot her qualms, her eyes shining with evangelistic light as she accompanied Paul through the empty rooms of Combe Farm, all personal feelings put aside as she made copious notes on the tour. Once she'd gained the overall picture she went through the house with Paul again, room by room, making suggestions, asking opinions, receptive of his ideas, but blunt with her opposition when she felt some of them were on the flash side for the character of the house.

Afterwards they sat on a rickety rustic bench in the sunshine while Eliza gave him a run-down on what she felt the house needed.

'In my opinion the hall lets the rest of the house down as it stands. Of course if you don't feel like replacing the staircase——'

'It's a great idea,' he said instantly. 'Giles wanted it out from the start.' He grinned. 'And he's too big to argue with! Besides, the hall's pretty naff as it is.'

'Once it's paved with stone slabs, and you've got carved banisters curving down the stair-well, you'll see an enormous difference.'

Paul listened to her suggestions with gratifying attention, but looked blank when she asked him for one word to describe his own idea of a theme for the house. He thought for a moment, then eyed her sheepishly.

'I was brought up in a council flat, but my mum was mad on stately homes. When I was a kid she dragged me to anybody's country seat she could pay to get into. As I got older I realised they all had this one thing in common, a sort of look, as though they'd been there forever. Know what I mean? *That*'s what I want for Combe Farm.'

'Timeless,' said Eliza briskly.

'That's the word! Timeless.' Paul leered suddenly, putting her on her guard. 'By the way, sweetheart, I'll give you a free hand in the rest of the house, but I've set my heart on a four-poster in my bedroom, with a nice big mirror lining the roof thing.'

'As you wish.' Suppressing a shudder, Eliza made a note of it. 'Now downstairs,' she went on determinedly, 'how about a tranquil, classical theme for the drawing-room? Lots of comfortable chairs and sofas and a few fringed rugs scattered on a pale carpet, small tables of the original period if I can hunt some down. And because the dining-room's on the small side I suggest making it darker, more intimate, painted with a palazzo finish in a sombre sort of shade, verdigris or amber, with gilt-framed mirrors, a couple of good oils.' She began packing her notes into her briefcase. 'I'll draw up floor plans, devise a scheme and show you a colour-board and furniture layout as soon as possible, plus brochures of bathrooms and kitchens, of course.'

Paul was impressed, and said so in no uncertain terms, then looked at his watch. 'Hell. I've got to rush.' He shook her hand again, holding on to it rather too long. 'Pity I can't stay while you do your survey, Eliza.'

She detached her hand without fuss. 'I work fastest alone,' she assured him. Paul ducked into the front seat of his Ferrari, then leaned out of the window, a look of such blatant familiarity in his eyes that all her worst fears were confirmed.

'By the way, Liza, it's time I came clean. I know your little secret. Not that I mind, love—to be honest I was tickled pink when I found out it was you, not Gem, the night of my party.'

Eliza stiffened. She stared down into Paul Wright's knowing, handsome face, feeling the colour leach from her own. She stepped back, her chin lifting.

'Gemma told you, I suppose.'

'No fear. She thinks I'm still in the dark.' He winked. 'Crikey, but you were good. I never sussed that night—must have been a bit over the top with the old bubbly. By the way, in case you're wondering, love, I only found out recently.'

'How?'

'Oh, come on, Liza—use the old grey matter! Mind, I don't know why you stood in for Gem that night but I'd bet her stomach upset was involved somewhere—but I won't press you.' He gave her a wide, white grin, then with one of his lightning switches of mood asked her how soon he could expect her scheme for his house.

'You want me to carry on with it?' asked Eliza stiffly.

He looked blank. 'Why not?'

'You might doubt my professional capabilities now you know I'm capable of the odd flash of insanity.'

He shook his head. 'Not on your life. Between you and me, love, it adds spice to the whole project. By the way—no need for Gemma to know I cottoned on. Our little secret, OK? Yours and mine.' And with another conspiratorial wink he drove off, leaving Eliza burning to tell him exactly what he could do with his plans for Combe Farm.

Knowing this was impossible for a variety of reasons, she set to work, her anger mounting as it dawned on her how Paul must have discovered the truth. If he hadn't found out at his party, and Gemma hadn't told him, only one other person knew she'd taken Gemma's place that night.

'How did you get on with Paul today?' asked Giles when he rang later that evening.

'Like a house on fire,' she said shortly.

There was silence for a moment.

'Nevertheless I detect a certain frost in the air, Eliza. Was Paul difficult?'

'On the contrary. Paul approved most of my suggestions. Of course, whether he'll approve of the extortionate price he'll have to pay is another story.'

'I can't see any difficulty on that score.' There was a pause. 'What's wrong, Eliza? Did something happen to upset you at Combe Farm today?'

'Yes. You could say that.'

'Tell me,' he ordered.

'After talking furniture and colour schemes for two hours Paul fired a rather shattering parting shot.' Eliza breathed in deeply. 'He knows it was me the night of his party.'

Giles cursed under his breath.

'You may well swear,' she said passionately. 'How *could* you, Giles?'

'*What*! What are you talking about——?'

'Do you think I'm an idiot? I *can* count! Gemma didn't tell him, I didn't tell him. That leaves you.'

'Why the hell would I do that?' he demanded, incensed.

'You tell me! What a fool I've been. I should have known you were just biding your time. Ever since we met up again you've been waiting to pounce, to make me pay for the dent I once made in your precious male ego. I just hope your revenge was sweet, Giles!' Eliza's voice cracked on the last and to her utter mortification she burst into tears.

'Eliza!' yelled Giles. 'Listen——'

'Go to hell!' she screamed, and slammed down the phone, then took it off the hook and ran into her bedroom to throw herself down on her bed, crying her eyes out with an abandon totally out of proportion to the gravity of the offence. It was all too trivial for words, she assured herself passionately, and eventually, sodden and exhausted, feeling as though she'd been run over by a bus, Eliza washed her face, made herself a cup of strong black coffee and put the phone back on the hook for a moment or two before dialling to leave a message on Gemma's answerphone.

Afterwards Eliza sat slumped on her sofa, staring at the sunset light pouring through the dormer windows. It was only natural to cry after such an embarrassing experience, of course. Anyone would. But it wasn't the real reason. She'd been in love with Giles Randolph all her adult life. For a while after her brother's wedding she'd persuaded herself she was cured, that the fire was out and the ashes cold. But one look at Giles at Paul's party had been enough to reactivate the embers into fiery life again. And now she was as hopelessly in love as she'd ever been, so much so that the thought of him, laughing with Paul behind her back, cut her to pieces.

When the phone rang a moment later she eyed it malevolently, then, afraid it might be Gemma, picked up the receiver.

'Eliza—don't hang up,' commanded Giles.

'I've got nothing to say to you,' she said hoarsely.

Giles cursed audibly. 'Will you listen to me, woman? I don't know what this is all about——'

'Liar!'

'I'm not in the habit of lying,' he said, his voice harsh with fury. 'You're behaving like a child——'

'I wish I were a child,' she choked, 'then none of this would have h-happened.'

'*Eliza*——'

She crashed the phone down on the handset, fought her tears into submission then went off to make yet more coffee. When the phone rang again she leapt across the room to answer it, but to her intense, mortifying disappointment it was Gemma, newly returned from wining and dining with Paul.

Gemma, fizzing with enthusiasm and happiness, told her twin that Paul was very impressed with Eliza's ideas for his house. 'So much impressed he says he won't bother to consult anyone else, Liza.'

'How nice,' said Eliza huskily, trying to sound enthusiastic.

'Hey,' said Gemma sharply. 'Have you been crying, Liza? Has Lawrence been upsetting you?'

'No.' Eliza hesitated, then shrugged, deciding to tell the truth. 'As a matter of fact I had a tiff with Giles.'

'With *Giles*?'

'Yes. Giles Randolph, friend of Rob, one-time object of our girlish passions, and victim of your darling little prank,' said Eliza viciously.

There was a lengthy pause.

'Liza,' said Gemma at last, her voice carefully neutral. 'If he made you cry, is it possible he's still the object of *your* passion?'

'Certainly not!' snapped Eliza.

'So what did you row about?'

'What does anyone row about? Not that it matters. My share of the work on his house is finished so I don't need to see him any more.'

With quite remarkable forbearance Gemma managed to refrain from pursuing the subject, reverting instead to her pleasure over Eliza's triumph in winning such a plum job from Paul. 'He's always in the tabloids, poor love, so you're bound to get masses of publicity. You'll be in one of those glossy magazines, with a picture of you as the rising young interior designer, alongside shots of Paul's country hideaway.'

'Charmian *will* be pleased!'

'Aren't you, love?'

'Ecstatic,' Eliza assured her. 'I'm very lucky. Now tell me about this shoot you're rushing off to tomorrow. Fur coats in the Seychelles?'

Gemma giggled. 'No. Evening gowns in the Shetlands. You'll probably see me in a Bruce Oldfield, cuddling a sheep! But the timing's perfect. Paul's in the States for a few days, so I might as well be off somewhere earning a crust instead of languishing alone while he's gone.'

Since Gemma had never languished alone in her entire life as far as Eliza could remember, she teased her sister a little as expected, wished her *bon voyage* and went to bed. But not to sleep.

Over the next few days Eliza plunged heart and soul into getting an entire scheme for Combe Farm ready by the time Paul returned to the UK.

'Charmian,' said Eliza one day, when everyone else was out of earshot. 'When the curtains arrive for Giles

Randolph's place, could someone else drive over to Little Rencombe and hang them for me?'

Charmian's eyebrows rose. 'I thought he was a chum of yours!'

'So did I.' Eliza looked bleak for a moment, then smiled coaxingly. 'Is that all right with you?'

'Of course, if you really feel you can't.'

'Thank you. Anyway, I need to concentrate on the order for Mr Wright.'

'By which I gather Giles Randolph is very much Mr Wrong.'

'Right!' Eliza attempted an unsuccessful laugh. 'Thank you, Charmian. I'd rather not run into Giles again for a bit. Or even forever.'

With Gemma out of the country and no encounters with Giles to look forward to, Eliza found life bleak. Now there was no prospect of seeing Giles at all she found herself longing for his company, and despised herself for her weakness. To stiffen her backbone she deliberately allowed the spectre of his laughter with Paul to haunt her, the thought of it acting like salt on a raw wound, not least because she would have gambled her last penny that her secret was safe with Giles Randolph. One way and another Eliza felt so thoroughly miserable that she surprised Lawrence considerably by accepting when he rang to invite her to the cinema one evening.

The film was entertaining, the supper following it pleasant, and Lawrence very careful to keep in her good graces. The entire evening was so much better than sitting at home waiting for the phone to ring that Eliza said yes a second time when Lawrence asked her if she fancied going to a party one of the faculty at his college was giving at the weekend.

'It's a bit off the beaten track—out Harcombe way,' he said as they parted. 'Know the area?'

'Quite well,' admitted Eliza. Harcombe was only a mile or two from Little Rencombe. And Giles. She smiled brightly. 'It's a longish drive. We'd better make an early start.'

'Splendid!' said Lawrence, plainly flattered by her enthusiasm. 'Seven-thirty, then?'

'Fine. Thank you for a nice evening, Lawrence.'

He moved towards her, his intention plain. When she retreated instinctively his eyes flashed angrily for a moment before he schooled his handsome, sulky face to acceptance. 'I thought you might have been otherwise engaged,' he said pointedly.

'If you mean with Giles, he's just a friend of my brother's.'

'He looked a damn sight more than that the night I met him, Eliza!'

'Just his manner,' she assured him airily, and sent him on his way, the merest mention of Giles sufficient to spoil all her pleasure in the evening.

To cheer herself up she went out to buy a new dress as a morale-booster in her lunch hour next day, defiantly choosing something very different from anything currently in her wardrobe. Charmian was loud with her approval of the silk jersey sheath, which was prohibitively expensive for a garment which in the hand looked rather like a long black vest, except for three rows of narrow black silk ribbon sewn chevron-fashion from shoulder to hip.

'Gemma's sort of thing, rather than mine,' said Eliza, eyeing the low neckline in doubt, but Charmian assured her the dress had tremendous style, worth every penny of whatever Eliza had paid for it.

When the buzzer sounded to announce Lawrence's arrival to take her to the party Eliza pressed the release button and returned to the mirror to check her appearance, biting her scarlet bottom lip at the sight of herself in the figure-hugging dress. To complement it she'd curled her hair and gathered it up in a loose cluster on the crown of her head, and fastened a cascade of baroque faux pearl drops to her earlobes. Oh, why not? she said defiantly to her reflection. She was bored with being the sensible Markham twin.

A quiet tap on her door sent her hurrying to fling it wide. She stood rooted to the spot, astounded. Instead of Lawrence, Giles confronted her, looking tired and dark-shadowed about the jaw, and overpoweringly tall in black corduroys and a black roll-neck sweater. His eyes narrowed as he took in her outfit. Without a word he kicked the door shut behind him and advanced on her, a pulse throbbing beside his mouth.

'Giles!' She eyed him with hostility. 'What brings you here? I was expecting someone else.'

'Obviously!'

'Is there something wrong?'

'There's been "something wrong" since our last little telephone discussion,' he said harshly. 'I didn't bother to ring again. I knew you'd slam the phone down the minute you heard my voice. So I've come in person to clear up a certain little misunderstanding.'

'But I don't want—I mean, you can't stay!' she said hurriedly, backing away. 'Lawrence will be here in a minute——'

'To hell with Lawrence!' He looked her up and down for a moment then without warning pulled her into his arms roughly and silenced her gasp of outrage with his mouth. Ignoring her struggles, he controlled her easily with one relentless arm, his free hand cupping her bottom to ram her hard against his hips.

Eliza, senses reeling, dimly heard the buzzer on her intercom, the noise prolonged as though someone was keeping a finger on the button in the street. She struggled, and Giles released her very slowly, trailing his lips down her throat as he set her free to go to the door.

'Eliza?' said Lawrence over the intercom. 'I'm here.'

'Come on up,' she said breathlessly, then caught sight of herself in the mirror, horrified at the damage Giles had done in a few short seconds.

'Let him in and keep him talking,' she told him curtly and fled to the bedroom.

When she emerged Giles was offering Lawrence a drink, playing the man in possession with such aplomb she could have hit him.

'Lawrence here tells me you're off to a party at the Wentworths' in Harcombe, Eliza,' he remarked. 'I've met them once or twice since my move to Tithe Barn.'

'How nice for you,' she said tightly, and smiled at Lawrence, who was staring at her like a man in shock.

'Eliza!' he said at last, awed. 'You look quite— quite wonderful.'

'So do you,' she returned with perfect truth. Lawrence, in wine-red jacket and white trousers, with a black silk cravat tied at the neck of his aquamarine shirt, was a work of art. 'I feel positively dowdy beside you!'

'In that dress?' said Giles. 'Be warned, Lawrence. You'll be fighting off every man in sight.'

'At a party full of cerebral academics? Surely not,' returned Eliza, colour high. 'Must rush you, Giles. It's time Lawrence and I were off.'

'Sorry to hold you up,' he said, blatantly insincere.

'Not at all. Goodbye.'

Lawrence echoed her, patently relishing the contrast with his previous encounter with Giles.

'Nice to meet you again, Shaw,' said Giles affably. 'See you soon, Eliza.'

Not, thought Eliza watching him run lightly down the stairs, if I see you first.

Still on fire from Giles's attentions but determined not to let the fact spoil her evening, Eliza showed far more warmth than usual to Lawrence on the journey to Harcombe. On their arrival at the Wentworths' house she found her reception mixed in equal proportions. The men swarmed round her at once, prowling like predators, while the women eyed Lawrence's companion with expressions ranging from envy to undisguised resentment. Eliza, in rather less than festive mood one way and another, accepted a glass of fruit punch to cheer herself up, discovered it had a kick like a mule and kept to plain fruit juice thereafter out of sheer self-preservation. Punch, she decided, was the exact word for the effect on far too many of the guests, some of whom had obviously visited the punch bowl several times before her arrival.

Eliza had hoped for an intellectual, stimulating evening among people who, with the exception of some of the wives, were uniformly academic in their interests. She was doomed to disappointment from the first. Relieved of the responsibility of bettering

student minds for an evening, the nearest most of the
men came to intellectual anecdote were racy accounts
of wild adventures in their own student days. And the
buffet supper provided by their hostess was as frugal
as the drink was plentiful, with the inevitable results.
As the party grew progressively rowdier Eliza found
herself fending off overtures which grew less and less
subtle, the *coup de grâce* given to the evening when
her hostess went off to answer the door and returned,
blazing with triumph, to usher a latecomer to the
revels.

'Look, everyone,' cried Dawn Wentworth. 'Meet a
new neighbour of ours—Giles Randolph.'

Gleaming blue eyes met Eliza's as Dawn
Wentworth's female friends converged on the new ar-
rival like bees to a honeypot. She turned away to find
Lawrence at her elbow, bristling with suppressed fury.

'What the hell is *he* doing here?' he demanded in
a fierce undertone.

'Search me,' said Eliza wearily.

'Lawrence!' boomed Malcolm Wentworth, beck-
oning them towards the new guest. 'Bring Eliza to
meet Giles Randolph. He's not long moved into the
area. Jolly clever barn conversion he's done, too.'

'We've met,' said Lawrence sourly. 'He's a friend
of Eliza's family.'

'I've known Eliza since she was knee-high—she's
very talented,' explained Giles blandly, who was no
longer dark-shadowed and dishevelled. Hair gleaming
like gilt in the semi-gloom of the Wentworths' party
lighting, his black and gold Paisley silk waistcoat worn
open over a crisp white shirt and black linen trousers,
he drew every female eye with an ease which inflamed

Lawrence with resentment he'd drunk too much punch to hide.

'He means she's an interior designer,' said Lawrence, grinding his teeth.

'Giles commissioned me to work on his house,' said Eliza hastily.

'You can work me over any time you like,' chimed in another of Lawrence's colleagues, grinning. 'Come and dance with me, you gorgeous designing hussy!'

The Wentworths' house boasted a large Victorian conservatory. For the moment it was crammed with dancers who'd imbibed so freely that the music was little more than an excuse for some extra-marital groping in the dim light. Eliza's partner seemed possessed of more tentacles than an octopus, and after only a minute or two she escaped his clutches by pleading a visit to the bathroom, where she locked herself in for a much needed respite from Giles, Lawrence and the world in general.

She applied lipstick with an unsteady hand, wondering how in the world Giles had managed to turn up at the Wentworths' right on cue. It would do him precious little good, she decided, snapping her evening purse shut. As soon as she could she'd drag Lawrence away from his colleagues and leave Giles to the feverish clutches of Dawn Wentworth and her pals. Which would serve him right.

Eliza spent a miserable hour frustrating all Giles's efforts to speak to her in private, which wasn't too difficult. Most of the time he was hedged in by a ring of women vying avidly for his attention. By midnight her social smile felt pinned to her face and she could take no more. Without ceremony she interrupted Lawrence's conversation with a dashing blonde divorcee bent on consoling him for his present semi-detached state.

'You can't want to leave yet!' Lawrence scowled. 'It's early.'

'Right,' said Eliza, shrugging. 'You stay. I'll call a cab.'

'Oh, no, you don't,' he said, grabbing her by the hand. 'I'm not letting you out of my sight.'

'Then let me drive, Lawrence—you've had too much to drink.'

'Rot!' Impatiently he hauled her over to their hosts to say their goodbyes. Eliza cringed inside at the look on Giles's face when Malcolm Wentworth winked and nudged, clapping Lawrence on the back as he assured him he'd be off home himself if he had a girl like Eliza to take to bed.

Giving Giles a cool little smile by way of goodnight, Eliza escaped from the house with a resentful Lawrence, then sat rigid with nerves in his car as he gunned it away from the house like a racing-driver first off the grid. She tried hard to keep calm, reassuring herself that the country route was deserted at this hour, but the rain was sheeting down in the pitch darkness and it was no night for the speed Lawrence was maintaining. Not drunk precisely, he was in the type of dangerous mood when any form of protest was useless. Eliza forced herself to keep silent for a mile or two as he made racing changes on corners and drove at a pace which frightened her to death, but after a while she couldn't bear it a minute longer.

'For heaven's sake slow *down*, Lawrence!'

'I'll do better than that,' he said thickly, and swerved the car off the road on to the grass verge. 'Come here!' he said and grabbed her.

Eliza was too thunderstruck to protest for a moment as Lawrence's mouth ground into hers, but when he jerked her seatbelt free and began crawling all over her she came to life and began fighting him off. He moaned with excitement and grabbed her flailing hands, showing surprising strength from someone she'd always regarded as just a little effete. He held her still with ominous ease, her struggles inflaming him all the more as he freed one hand to thrust it into her dress, groping for her breasts. With a screech of disgust Eliza arched back in the seat, managing to get rid of one of his hands only to find another searching under her skirt as Lawrence panted lurid threats of what he was about to do to her. Incensed, Eliza gave a frantic, superhuman heave and shoved at him, feeling something tear as she yanked herself free. Beside herself with rage, she clouted Lawrence violently on the nose with her clenched fist, bringing a howl of fury from him as his blood spouted in a hot sickly stream down his chin.

Eliza seized her advantage. Grabbing her small evening bag, she wrenched open the door, leapt from the car and ran for her life into the wet darkness, every nerve straining to escape. She could hear him stumbling after her for a while, calling her name in hysterical rage. But Lawrence had drunk more punch than was wise, and Eliza knew of old that he was sickened by blood, his own or anyone else's. Nausea would soon slow him down.

Eliza cursed the lightning spotlighting her flight, then realised she needed it to find the telephone box she'd noticed on the way to the party. Keeping to the edge of the road, she peered from side to side as lightning flashes lit up the darkness more and more frequently. With a pause every now and then to listen for footsteps between peals of thunder, she stumbled on down the lonely dark road, tears mingling with the rain on her face as she cursed the entire male sex.

Then through a lull in the storm she heard a car. Without hesitation she leapt into the ditch, oblivious of the brambles which tore at her as she flattened herself out of sight. Hardly daring to breathe, she waited, heart thumping, praying Lawrence would drive past, but the car halted and stood idling, and after a while, cursing a capricious fate, she gritted her teeth and climbed wearily from the ditch, wincing as brambles scratched her legs.

'Oh, all right, Lawrence, but if you try any more caveman nonsense——' She gave a sudden gasp of horror as lightning lit the male figure bending to give her a hand. *'Giles!'*

'Yes. Giles.' He yanked her out of the ditch without ceremony and pushed her into his car, then sprinted round it to get in the driving seat. 'I've just left Lawrence bleeding like a stuck pig, and feeling very sorry for himself, one way and another,' he said grimly as he drove off.

Eliza huddled shivering in her seat, casting a searching look at his stony profile as the lightning lit up the night. 'What did you do to him?' she asked suspiciously.

'Why do you always think the worst of me, Eliza? I didn't do anything to the fool.' He sent a cold, unamused look in her direction. 'You'd already done more than enough from what little I could make out.

Lawrence was not only bloody, but incoherent and threatening to throw up.'

Eliza's teeth chattered. 'I d-don't suppose you'd d-drive me home?'

'You suppose right. I won't. I'm not driving all the way to Pennington and back on a filthy night like this. You can stay the night at Tithe Barn. Lawrence can bloody well stay where he is all night, as far as I'm concerned.'

Anger radiated from Giles like infra-red rays, deciding Eliza to keep her head down and say nothing on the short journey to Little Rencombe. When they arrived Giles hauled her out of the car and pushed her up the steps, catching her by the arm impatiently when she stumbled. He unlocked the door, then thrust her into the darkness of the great room, which blossomed into a familiar, welcoming haven as Giles switched on lamps, one by one.

Eliza stood like Lot's wife, enduring the appalled scrutiny Giles turned on her. She had no need of a mirror to know what he was seeing; hair coming down in rats' tails, mascara and lipstick in blotches, one earring missing. Her hand went up instinctively to the neckline of her dress to hold the tear together over her breasts, and as though the movement released him from a spell Giles leapt towards her, seizing her by the wrists to hold her arms wide.

'What happened, Eliza?' he demanded fiercely, his eyes blazing as they registered the torn dress and the bloodstains on her scratched legs. 'What did the swine do to you? *Answer* me!'

Now she was safe and relatively warm Eliza wanted nothing more than to cast herself against his chest and go to sleep. 'He didn't rape me,' she said baldly, too tired to choose her words.

'From the look of you he had a bloody good try!' He pushed her across the room to a sofa. 'Sit there for a minute while I get you a drink.'

Eliza swallowed brandy obediently, the fiery spirit taking her breath away as it did its work. She gave him a small, polite smile, then handed him the glass.

'Thank you so much. I feel better now—could I have a wash?'

'All in good time,' Giles stood, arms folded, his eyes relentless. 'First I want to know exactly what happened. Afterwards you can have a hot bath and go to bed.'

Eliza, with such a heavenly prospect as incentive, described Lawrence's attack as rapidly and succinctly as possible, looking anywhere but up at Giles.

'What the devil did the bastard think he was doing?' he demanded, with a cold violence which put paid to Eliza's brandy-fuelled warmth.

It was difficult to control her chattering teeth. 'He thought he was making love to me. He's wanted to for ages, but I've never let him, you see,' she said simply. 'Fortunately he'd had too much to drink, so I managed to punch him on the nose and escape.'

'Where did you imagine you were escaping *to*?' he demanded grimly. 'Here, by any chance?'

'No!' Her eyes flashed. 'Certainly not. As it happens I remembered seeing a telephone box on the journey over. I thought I could ring for a taxi to pick me up.'

Giles gave her a pitying look. 'Did you honestly expect one to come all the way out here after midnight in a storm like this?' He shook his head. 'And I thought Gemma was the brainless one!'

She hugged her arms across her chest in sudden fury. 'It wasn't my fault Lawrence went berserk!'

Giles's mouth curved with distaste as he eyed her up and down. 'If that dress is yours I disagree. I suggest you get yourself upstairs and strip it off before you get pneumonia. Can you manage under your own steam?'

'Yes, thank you,' she said with what dignity she could muster. She hobbled upstairs ahead of him, then turned in the guest-room doorway. 'Where's Poppy?'

'At the kennels. I've been away.' Giles brushed past her into the bathroom to turn the hot water on full. 'No more talk. In there—now!'

Once he'd gone Eliza stripped off her clothes and climbed wearily into the bath, wishing she could stay in the soothing water indefinitely. But if she did she'd fall asleep, and then Giles would probably barge in and haul her out. And she was in enough trouble for one night. She dragged herself out of the bath, rinsed out her underthings and hung them with her dress to dry. She swathed a towel round her wet hair, another round herself toga-fashion and went out into the bedroom, to find Giles waiting for her.

'Better?'

She nodded. 'Much.'

'I've brought you a sweatshirt and dressing-gown—best I can do.'

'Thank you.' She mustered a polite smile. 'I'll join you downstairs in a minute. I suppose you won't change your mind and drive me home, by any chance?'

'No, I will not!' He hung on to his temper with visible difficulty. 'The only place you're going tonight is bed. I'll go down and make some tea. After I've seen to that cut.'

Eliza looked down at the blood seeping into the white towel from a small gash on her chest, then forced herself to stand still as Giles applied a dressing with hands not altogether steady.

'Wrap yourself up and come downstairs,' he ordered without looking at her, and went from the room.

Eliza stared at the door despairingly as it closed behind him. What a disaster of a night!

CHAPTER NINE

FEELING ridiculous in her engulfing borrowed plumes, Eliza went downstairs on bare feet to find Giles adding logs to the fire he'd lit in the big stone fireplace.

'Come and sit near the fire.' He installed her on the sofa he'd drawn up to the hearth, then turned to a tray on a nearby table. 'I've made some sandwiches. The Wentworths obviously don't believe in feeding their guests.'

'I don't——' she began, but his cold, quelling stare put an end to her protest. He sat beside her, vigilant, as she forced down a mouthful or two before drinking the hot, reviving tea.

'You obviously think I'm to blame for what happened,' she said at last, breaking the silence.

'To a certain extent, yes.' His eyes gleamed cold with distaste. 'If you persist in wearing dresses which expose too much of your—person, any man with blood in his veins will want to touch as well as look.'

Eliza shot him a glowering look. 'So it's all my fault!'

Giles shrugged. 'Tonight, yes. Last time, at Paul's party, a lot of the blame was Gemma's. But take my advice, Eliza. In future avoid dresses which cling so faithfully.'

Her face flamed. 'Thanks a lot. You certainly know how to make a girl feel attractive, Giles Randolph!'

'You know perfectly well you're attractive,' he said roughly. 'Why the hell do you think Lawrence's pals were circling round you like vultures tonight? Or why Paul Wright was pawing the ground the other day?'

Eliza clenched her fists. 'Lawrence's pals were drunk. Paul's reason is my resemblance to Gemma.'

Giles gave a derisive snort of laughter. 'Don't be so stupid, Eliza.'

'You're right. I *am* stupid,' she agreed fiercely. 'For one thing I just can't figure out how you managed to appear at the Wentworths' party tonight.'

'I could tell my arrival came as an unpleasant surprise.'

'Only to me. Every other woman there was sickeningly ecstatic!'

'Jealous, Eliza?'

'That'll be the day!'

Giles shrugged, turning away to stare into the fire. 'It's no mystery. I told you I'd met the Wentworths.'

'You said nothing about being invited to the party.'

'I wasn't.' He gave her a cynical, sidelong glance. 'They've asked me round several times, but I've always made some excuse. Tonight I simply rang them and invited them round *here* for a drink. Dawn Wentworth was agonised at not being able to accept and implored me to go to their party. Exactly as I anticipated.'

'How simple,' she said with sarcasm. 'But that only explains *how* you came to be there. Would you mind telling me why?'

'It was the last thing I felt like doing,' he said wearily. 'I only got back from Scotland this morning, then I drove to London on another errand, and afterwards drove down to see you. When you wouldn't let me talk to you I saw red. So I did a spot of gate-crashing at the Wentworths' gathering, determined to collar you there. But you avoided me like the plague all night then took off early, so I was frustrated again.' He turned to look her in the eye. 'By no means a new experience where you're concerned.'

Eliza coloured painfully, and turned away to stare into the flames.

'Since you were the reason I went to the blasted party, there was precious little point in staying once you'd left,' he went on. 'Besides, I didn't like the look of Lawrence. The state he was in I was afraid he'd have you both in a ditch, or worse, so I followed you as soon as I could escape Dawn Wentworth's clutches.'

She turned to look at him in surprise. 'Did you actually see me run from the car?'

He shook his head, his face set. 'No. I saw the car on the verge and went to investigate. When I found Lawrence covered with blood I thought there'd been an accident, but a short, sharp bout of persuasion soon had the story out of him, after which I drove off to look for you. Luckily you hadn't got very far.'

Eliza got to her feet. 'I apologise for putting you to so much trouble,' she said dully. 'If you don't mind I'll take myself off to bed, out of your way. In the morning I'll ring for a taxi——'

Giles sprang to his feet, one eyebrow raised. 'Don't you think a taxi might prove difficult? You don't have any clothes to wear.'

'If you can provide me with needle and thread I shall manage!'

'Manage what?' He paused. 'You can't mean to mend that dress.'

'I certainly do. Enough to get me home, anyway.'

He shrugged indifferently. 'As you like.'

'Right. I'll go to bed, then.' Eliza turned to make for the stairs.

'Not so fast.' Giles caught her by the arm. 'Before you do you can damn well listen to what I've been trying to tell you from the moment I first saw you this evening. You were wrong, Eliza. Paul found out about the masquerade right enough, but *not* through me.'

Eliza shook off his hand violently. 'No one else knew. How could he have found out if you didn't tell him?'

His eyes locked with hers. 'Think back to the day he walked in on you in the kitchen here. Remember the way you were dressed at the time?'

'Yes, of course—in one of the jumpsuits I use for dirty work.'

'But when Paul arrived you were hot and very much unzipped, I gather.'

Eliza flushed. 'How do you know that?'

'Paul was very explicit,' said Giles grimly. 'It seems he'd swallowed the story of lost weight at first, but when he surprised you that day the penny dropped. He'd been with Gemma the night before, remember, so this time Paul, who by no means lacks grey matter, put two and two—or shall we say one and one?— together.'

'When did Paul tell you all this?' she asked dully.

'This very day, Eliza. I tried to contact him the moment you let fly with your accusations, but he was away. I had to wait until he got back.' Giles held her eyes steadily. 'This afternoon I asked him straight out who'd spilled the beans but he assured me no one had. He figured it out all by himself. Ask him, if you doubt my word.'

Eliza stood very still, her eyes riveted to the cold accusation in his. 'It seems I owe you an apology. Again. I'm sorry. I jumped to the wrong conclusion.'

'As you tend to do where I'm concerned.' His eyes hardened. 'But Paul told me something else, too, Eliza.'

'Go on.'

'My instinct was right. It's the differences between the Markham twins which titillate him, not the resemblance. He's infatuated with Gemma, all right, but at the same time he's very much drawn to certain things about you.'

Eliza's eyes blazed. 'Namely a few extra inches round the bust, I suppose!'

'More or less. By the way,' he added, 'if you switch with Gemma again I advise wearing a high-necked dress. Paul took great pleasure in telling me you possess a small mole between your breasts.'

Eliza gasped. 'Gem's dress wasn't that indecent!'

'Not so the unzipped boiler-suit, it seems. Paul says Gemma doesn't have a mole,' stated Giles, poker-faced. 'At least not in that particular location. Which is why he twigged. He thought back to the party, and the feel of you in his arms when he was crawling all over you on the dance floor——'

'He said *that*?'

'No. The phrase is mine. Paul was more euphemistic.'

'After this, how am I supposed to work with him on Combe Farm?' She ground her teeth impotently. 'Yet if I don't I'll lose such a magnificent order for Charmian.'

'Don't be ridiculous, Eliza, you're a professional. Of course you carry on with the job. When you see

Paul again you'll put all this from your mind and behave as though nothing had happened.' Giles frowned as he saw her cheeks suddenly wet with tears. 'What's this?'

'Sorry,' she said hoarsely. 'It's just that it's been such a horrible evening. I only went to the party with Lawrence because I thought a crowd of academics would be interesting. But none of the men wanted to *talk* to me. They just chatted me up or tried to touch me, and—and Lawrence didn't even mind! He was actually gratified that his mates found "the girl-friend" sexy. Then you turn up to make my joy complete, and to top it off you tell me Paul Wright thinks the only thing of note about me is my bust measurement!'

'Stop feeling so sorry for yourself.' Giles eyed the tears without sympathy for a moment, then with an impatient exclamation he pulled her into his arms, utterly demolishing Eliza's self-control. She sobbed wildly into his shoulder, barely noticing when he sat down on the sofa, holding her in his arms until the storm subsided. When she was calmer Giles mopped at her sodden face with a napkin from the tea-tray, and put a finger under her chin to look very hard into her swollen eyes.

'Before I let you get some rest I want the truth. Did Lawrence really fail in his rape attempt?'

Eliza nodded, sniffling inelegantly. 'Yes, of course he did. He tore my dress, and cut me with his signet ring, but nothing worse. My legs got scratched because I chose a ditch full of brambles to hide in.'

'He's lucky I didn't give him more than a bloody nose to worry about,' said Giles menacingly. He looked at her for a moment, his eyes inscrutable. 'Just so your cup runneth over, you'd better hear my other reason for chasing hotfoot to Pennington tonight to see you. You won't have any problem with Paul. I've sorted him out where you're concerned.'

She struggled upright, pushing her damp, untidy hair from her face. 'How?'

'By telling him he was trespassing.'

She frowned. 'On Lawrence's preserves?'

'No.' Giles smiled faintly. 'On mine.'

Eliza's jaw dropped. '*Yours*! What on earth made you say that?'

He shrugged. 'On the spur of the moment it seemed the simplest way to save trouble all round. It lets you carry on with Combe Farm happily, and Paul will go on putting work my way instead of taking umbrage if I'd blacked his eye—which I would have done if he'd gone on talking about your birthmark.'

'Oh.' Her eyes hardened. 'I see. How very expedient. This way you play knight errant and hang on to your business contacts at the same time.'

'Precisely.'

'He'll tell Gem the minute she gets back,' she warned him.

'He already has. Paul rang me before I left for the party to say Gemma was home a day early and was thrilled at the news. Now you can see why I needed to get a word in your ear so urgently, Eliza. I wanted to put you in the picture before she gets hold of you.'

Eliza jumped to her feet in a panic. 'What on earth am I to say when she does?'

Giles got up more slowly, stretching. 'Tell her that, despite the spanner she once threw in the works, the long-standing bond between you and me has strengthened during the time spent together over my house.' His eyes lit with a cynical gleam. 'Don't look so desperate! You can bow out of the arrangement the moment you feel it's safe to do so—when Paul's intentions towards Gemma are officially declared honourable, or until his cheque for your work on Combe Farm is safe in Charmian Lucas's pocket. Whichever seems more important to you. And in the meantime,' he added, looking suddenly very formidable, 'this temporary arrangement of ours will kill another bird with the same stone. Shall I tell Lawrence Shaw, or will you?'

'After what happened tonight I don't suppose I'll need to.' She stared at him, uncertain whether to smother Giles with gratitude, or give him hell for his interference.

Giles's hands reached out to steady her as she swayed suddenly. 'Shall I carry you to bed?'

Eliza could think of nothing she wanted more, but she shook her head.

'What's the matter?' he asked sharply. 'Do you feel ill?'

'No. Just tired.' She forced a smile. 'But not so tired I can't get to bed under my own steam.'

'Pity.'

Their eyes met.

Giles's mouth twisted. 'Don't worry. I'm not about to leap on you, demanding return on my investment.'

'I'm sure you're not,' she retorted tartly. 'After all, if you did I might hold you to this crazy marriage idea—and then where would you be, Giles Randolph?' Her shoulders drooped suddenly. 'Besides, the way I look at the moment I can hardly present much temptation.'

The dark blue eyes swept from her bare feet to her damp, tumbled hair in a hard, unnerving survey. 'For someone so clever at her job you can be extraordinarily dim-witted on occasion,' he said gratingly. 'For God's sake go to bed, Eliza.'

Something in his tone sent Eliza on her way without another word. Glad to be alone at last, she shut the bedroom door behind her, discarded the borrowed dressing-gown and crept into bed, dazed by the new turn of events. Giles must be losing his wits, she thought numbly. But now Paul had given the glad news to Gemma the fat was in the fire good and proper. Eliza sighed, and pummelled her pillow, hoping Gemma was still too wrapped up in her own romance to suspect that her sister's was not at all what it seemed.

After tossing and turning until dawn Eliza fell so heavily asleep that she had no idea where she was for a moment until her eyes focused blearily on Giles at the foot of the bed. Yawning, she struggled to sit up, holding the covers up to her nose as he set a mug of tea down on the bedside table. Giles, in pale cords and polished brogues, a Wedgwood-blue sweater over a striped yellow shirt, looked irritatingly well-groomed and brisk, barring smudges of fatigue the exact colour of his eyes.

'Good morning, Eliza. How do you feel?' he enquired.

'Shattered.'

He went over to the dressing-table to search in a drawer and turned round, brandishing a pair of beautifully laundered jeans. 'Eureka. Mrs Treasure told me these were here. You left them behind last time, so she dealt with them.'

'You needn't sound quite so desperate to get rid of me, Giles!'

'Quite the reverse,' he assured her, sitting on the edge of the bed. 'I just need you decently clothed in——' He consulted his watch. 'Let's say an hour, to be on the safe side. Our lunch guests will be here by then.'

'Our *what*?' shrieked Eliza, spilling her tea on the quilt.

Giles mopped at the stain with a handkerchief, un-ruffled. 'Paul rang earlier. He said Gemma was clam-ouring to talk to you, but I flatly refused to wake you up, so Paul insists on driving Gemma down from town to take us out to a celebratory lunch.'

'And you agreed? You're mad!' said Eliza wildly. 'Quite apart from a dozen other objections, what do I wear?'

'Those jeans. I'll find you something to go with them,' he said calmly. 'So get yourself up and in the mood right now. I didn't go to all this trouble to have you spoil my noble gesture, Eliza, so co-operate. I'll give you twenty minutes. Oh, by the way,' he added from the doorway, 'Mrs Treasure came round earlier. I gave her the glad tidings, too.'

Eliza groaned, head in hands, as Giles took himself off, whistling in a way which made her long to throw something at him.

Eliza spent most of the time allotted on her hair, which, she decided morosely at the end of it, could have done with a lot more. Abandoning it im-patiently, she dressed as far as the jeans, did what she could to her face with the lipstick and eye pencil which were all her small evening purse contained by way of beauty aids, then, wrapping herself in Giles's dressing gown, she went downstairs to find him removing wads of paper from the shoes she'd worn the night before. He held up the gleaming low-heeled black pumps for her approval.

'Mrs Treasure polished them for you.'

Eliza, the wind taken out of her sails, accepted them with thanks and slid them on her bare feet. 'Good. All I lack now is something to cover my top half.'

Giles nodded. 'Right. Come back upstairs, and we'll effect a transformation.'

'How?' she demanded scornfully.

'You'll be forced to enter my bedroom to find out,' he said suavely. 'But don't worry. My baser instincts are on a tight rein.'

She glared at him balefully as she followed him into his room.

'There.' He pointed to an array of boxes on his bed. 'You're the designer, Eliza. Create an effect with one of those.'

Eliza inspected the boxes, her ill-humour evaporating. 'Goodness, Giles, what exotic taste!' Amused, she held up a cream-dotted indigo silk shirt.

His lips twitched. 'Not guilty. It was a present from a lady.'

'I suppose I could wear it as a tunic, if you've got something I can use as a sash.' Eliza smiled at him with rather more warmth.

'At last, a smile,' he observed drily.

She flushed guiltily. 'Sorry, Giles. Last night made a dent in my sense of humour, one way and another. And while we're on the subject I do appreciate your motives in—well——'

'Laying claim to you?'

'I wouldn't have put it quite like that,' she muttered. 'Turn your back. Let's see if your idea works.'

The filmy shirt, although voluminous on Eliza, looked quite presentable cinched in at the waist with a navy silk scarf new from its gift-wrapping. She rolled up the shirt-sleeves, bloused out the folds above the scarf, and struck an exaggerated model pose.

'Well, how do I look?'

Giles turned round and whistled. 'Gemma'll be green with envy!' He surveyed her with leisurely approval, then frowned. 'I almost forgot. You'll need this to complete the picture.' He fished in his pocket for a small jeweller's box.

Eliza snapped it open to stare, transfixed, at a large baguette emerald flanked by two rose-cut diamonds on a heavy gold band. She swallowed. 'Giles! I can't possibly——'

'Why not? It's the first thing Gemma will look for.' He took the ring from the box and slid it on the third finger of her left hand. 'Hm, not bad. A bit loose, but not much.'

'But where did you get this at such short notice, for heaven's sake?'

'I keep it in the safe behind that mirror over there. It was my mother's.'

She sighed heavily. 'I don't know that I can cope with all this, Giles. It's such a terrible con.'

'Nonsense,' he said briskly. 'Just think of it as a means to an end. I admit it was sheer impulse which led me to say we were engaged. But on reflection it's not a bad idea.' His eyes met hers. 'Speaking for myself, it won't be any hardship to pretend I'm your lover for a while.'

Eliza looked away, colouring. 'I wish I knew why you were doing this.'

'If you think it's some roundabout way of insinuating myself into your bed, you're mistaken,' he said acidly. 'As I said last night, it just seemed like the best way to divert Paul's eyes from you to Gemma, and keep them there. At the same time he stays sweet about my business contacts, and you keep the contract for Combe Farm securely in your clever little hands.'

Eliza sighed, holding up her hand to let the stones in the ring catch the light. 'I just hope I don't put my foot in it some time. And this ring scares me rigid. What if I lose it?'

'You won't. Besides, it's insured.'

'But it was your mother's, Giles——'

'I wouldn't have had it on tap otherwise!'

The day grew more and more out of hand for Eliza as it wore on. When she went downstairs she found Mrs Treasure in the kitchen, waiting to present her with a great bunch of sweet williams to mark the occasion.

'Phyllis, how lovely. And thank you so much for washing my jeans.' Eliza bent her hot face to the flowers as Mrs Treasure expressed her delight at the news.

'I don't know if I can carry this off,' groaned Eliza later to Giles.

'Of course you can! And if nothing else it should convince Lawrence to stay out of your hair in future. The bastard had a lucky escape last night,' Giles added, his eyes darkening.

'From you?' she asked, surprised.

'Yes. From me.' Giles smiled evilly. 'I had a short talk with Lawrence before I went searching for you. I told him he'd have me to answer to if he bothered you again.'

She stared at him resentfully. 'I've managed to fight my own battles up to now perfectly well, you know, even without your assistance.'

'As I've said before,' said Giles acidly, 'it's an optimistic knight errant who hopes for gratitude.'

She smiled remorsefully. 'Sorry, Giles. I haven't been lavish with my thanks, have I?'

'A smile or two like that would make up the deficit,' he said lightly.

'Pity the curtains couldn't have been up to complete the picture,' she remarked, as they drank coffee at the kitchen table later among a welter of Sunday papers. 'I'd have liked Gemma to see the finished result.'

'She'll be down again often enough when it's completed.'

'I shouldn't think so.' Eliza looked up at Giles ruefully. 'Surely once all this nonsense is over you'll be glad to cross the Markham twins off your list!'

He shrugged. 'Not at all. This "nonsense", as you put it, is pure entertainment for the most part. And as I told you before, it's no hardship to pass as your fiancé for a while.'

Eliza, not sure how to respond to that, tried to concentrate on the papers, but after a while her eyes were drawn irresistibly from the page to the room.

Even without its curtains the vast kitchen at Tithe Barn was now a pleasant, comfortable place, the warm, gold-stippled walls and cool green tiles giving it exactly the summery atmosphere Eliza had been

aiming for. She felt a sudden sharp pang of possession as she pictured it with children running in and
out, the smell of good cooking in the air.

'Penny for your thoughts,' said Giles.

Eliza looked across to find him watching her. 'I
was congratulating myself on this kitchen. It looks
good—and will look even better once the curtains and
blinds are up. But you could do with some plants on
the windowsills and a few bunches of herbs and garlic
hanging——' She stopped, shrugging. 'Sorry. I get
carried away.'

'Don't be sorry. I agree on all counts.' He frowned
as the roar of a powerful car engine shattered the
quiet. 'Heigh-ho, all peace is at an end. Our visitors
have arrived.' He rose, reaching for Eliza's hand.
'Smile, woman. This is a celebration, not a wake!'

Gemma, in a white stretch jersey sheath few women
could have got away with, rushed to greet her sister,
arms outstretched, enveloping Eliza in a cloud of
perfume as she explained in a rush how she'd got
mixed up with the return date of her trip, and how
thrilled she was at Eliza's news.

'Well, well!' she said, giving Giles a guarded,
pleading smile. 'Congratulations, you lucky man.'

'I second that, mate,' said Paul with a wink, his
skin-tight jeans and new Italian leather jacket in
marked contrast to the lived-in elegance of his large
host. 'OK if I kiss the bride?'

'If she doesn't object,' said Giles, holding Eliza
firmly by the hand as she turned her cheek to the kiss
Paul aimed at her mouth.

'Come inside,' said Eliza quickly. 'You don't get
the chance to see much of my work, Gem—only this
isn't finished, of course.'

Her twin professed herself much impressed, aiming a teasing look at Giles as she exclaimed over the vast proportions of the main room. 'At least you won't crash into the chandelier here.'

Giles groaned as the sisters took pleasure in relating the story of the rugby international once watched by Rob and Giles in the Markham household.

'When England scored against France Giles leapt in the air and demolished the overhead light,' said Eliza, laughing. 'Mother was terribly cross.'

'So was my grandfather when I asked him for money to pay for the damage!' said Giles with feeling. 'He docked my pocket money accordingly until the debt was settled.'

'You're lucky you had any,' remarked Paul. 'The first money I ever got I earned myself.'

'Eliza!' said Gem hurriedly, pouncing on her sister's hand. 'What a ring! Oh, love, it's exquisite.'

Eliza looked up into blue, steady eyes over Gemma's artistically tousled curls.

'A beautiful ring for a beautiful lady,' Giles said calmly.

'How graceful!' Gemma fluttered her eyelashes at him. 'By the way, Mother was utterly delighted when I rang Rob to give the glad news.'

Eliza stared at her aghast. 'You've been on the line to *New Zealand*?'

'Never mind, darling.' Giles put an arm round her swiftly, giving her a warning squeeze. 'I know you wanted to tell them yourself——'

'Only I jumped in with both feet as usual,' said Gemma remorsefully. 'But when Giles wouldn't wake you up to talk to me I just had to speak to someone.'

Eliza felt numb on the way out to lunch. Giles's statement to Paul had been like a pebble tossed in a pool, sending ripples of reaction far and wide. Now her parents knew they'd be up to their ears in wedding plans and Rob would be organising leave to act as best man, because Giles Randolph had been Rob's friend long before getting engaged to Rob's sister. She gave herself a mental shake. But Giles wasn't engaged to her. Not really. As if he knew what she was thinking Giles put out a hand and covered her clasped fists, a gesture which provoked a sly instruction from Paul about keeping hands on the wheel and off Eliza.

The celebration lunch was a strain. Gemma was plainly uneasy in Giles's company, as Eliza had expected, and while Eliza responded with suitable gaiety to the toasts she found it impossible to enjoy the delicious food and the champagne in the circumstances, not least because Paul was in a strangely belligerent mood. He took obvious pleasure in embarrassing everyone present when Gemma discovered her sister's shirt actually belonged to Giles.

'You old skinflint!' jeered Paul. 'Buy the girl a new one. Money gets you everywhere with women, take it from me, mate.'

Gemma, flushing scarlet, sent him an incensed look of reproach, while Eliza, scenting danger in Giles's sudden stillness, plunged hastily into her plans for Combe Farm.

'Let's go there after lunch,' said Paul at once. 'You may as well see it now we're down here, Gem. OK with you, Giles?'

Giles agreed with cool courtesy, smiling in reassurance at Eliza as he took her hand on the way to the car. 'Don't worry. I won't queer your pitch at

Combe Farm after taking such pains to keep it for you, I promise.'

'He's in a funny mood today,' whispered Eliza.

'He can be an awkward customer sometimes,' warned Giles in an undertone. 'He didn't get to the top so fast without treading on a few toes en route, believe me—probably a few necks as well.'

To Eliza's relief Paul's pride in his new home made the rest of the afternoon less of a strain, his mood mellowing visibly as he led the way from room to room while Eliza outlined her ideas for each one.

'Isn't she clever?' said Gemma in admiration. 'What a showplace you'll have when it's finished, Paul.'

'You like it, love?' He grinned, proud as a child with a new toy.

Gemma assured him it was a dream house, then asked Giles to run them back to Tithe Barn. 'We'd better be on our way. I've been asked to a rather smart party tonight, and told to bring a gorgeous man, so I'm taking Paul.'

His sharp, handsome features smug with pleasure at her compliment, Paul leered as he helped her into the car. 'For you, love, anything!' Then without warning he spun round to seize Eliza by the waist, one hand splayed in deliberate familiarity below her breast as he grinned into her face. 'Be a sport—come with us, Liza! I fancy making an entry with a matched pair like you two.'

Giles, his face wooden, gave Paul a very straight look as Eliza detached herself and got in the car. 'Eliza's staying put tonight, I'm afraid. We're for a private celebratory dinner at home, just the two of us.'

'Not half!' said Paul with a wink. 'Don't blame you, mate. I'd do the same in your shoes—pour vintage bubbly down the girl, then take her to bed.'

Eliza was very silent once they'd waved the Ferrari out of sight.

'What's troubling you?' asked Giles as he followed her into the kitchen. He eyed her closely as she filled a kettle and put tea in a pot. 'It was hard going for you today, one way and another, I know.'

'I have a feeling this little charade of ours won't be needed long, Giles.' She turned to face him. 'Gemma can't possibly want to marry Paul, can she? He was a complete oaf today, showing off all the time. She's worth ten of him, no matter how much money he's got.'

'Love is an illogical emotion. Blind, too, where Gemma's concerned.'

'Do you think I should tell her he knows about the switch?'

'No. Stay out of it. I'd lay odds the magic's wearing off in any case.' Giles put his arm round her, tightening it a little as she leaned against him limply, making no objection to the embrace. 'But try not to worry, Eliza. If Gemma really is set on Paul you'll just have to grin and bear it.'

'I know.' She looked up at him ruefully. 'But it's difficult. Today he kept eyeing my—my front all the time; deliberately reminding me about my birthmark.'

'The catalyst which started all this.' Giles's eyes narrowed to an unsettling gleam. 'One, incidentally, I haven't seen for myself.'

She flushed. 'I'm not in the habit of displaying it.'

'Even to your fiancé?' he said lightly, releasing her. 'A title I hold with full Markham approval, I might add—barring yours.'

'Mine was never requested,' she reminded him, and turned away to make the tea.

CHAPTER TEN

AFTER they'd fetched Poppy from the kennels they took her for a long walk in the woods, then ate bacon and eggs at the kitchen table, a meal Eliza enjoyed far more than her lunch.

'A good thing Paul can't see us at our humble repast,' commented Giles. 'My stock with him would plummet.'

'Would that distress you?'

'No.' His eyes took on a steely glint. 'He bloody well got on my nerves today where you're concerned. A pity you work for Charmian Lucas. If you were self-employed I'd tell you to stuff his job.'

'It would hardly do my reputation much good however I'm employed,' she said tartly. 'It was you who told me to be professional on the subject, if you remember.'

He eyed her narrowly. 'Are you likely to spend much time alone there?'

'I shall make sure I don't. When there's a big job like this in hand we all pitch in, anyway.'

'Good.' Giles led her into the other room. 'I'll fetch some drinks and we'll listen to some music, or watch the play on Channel Four.'

'No, Giles, I must go home.'

'Leave it until morning. I'll get you there early enough to creep in before anyone else turns up.'

Eliza shook her head. 'I need some time to myself. I've got a heavy day tomorrow, so I'd rather sleep in my own little bed, thanks just the same.'

'I wasn't suggesting you slept in mine!'

'I didn't think you were.' She flashed him a resentful look. 'This engagement is only a pretence, after all. You made your views on marriage very plain!'

'If it were for real,' said Giles conversationally, sitting down beside her, 'how would you react if I did want to take you to bed?'

Eliza stared at the seascape above the fireplace, her pulse racing. 'Since it's not for real, there's no point in speculating.' She started up, but Giles pulled her back gently, slid his arm round her shoulders and turned her face up to his.

'Answer me, Eliza.'

Her lids dropped like shutters to hide the alarm in her eyes. 'Since it isn't real, there's no point in discussing it.'

Giles was silent for so long that Eliza looked up at last to surprise a very strange expression in the intent blue eyes. He smiled slowly. 'All right, let's put it another way. Do you find me physically repulsive?'

She looked away. 'No, I don't. No woman has ever found you physically repulsive—and well you know it.'

'I suppose that's what I wanted to hear.' He tapped an admonishing finger on her cheek. 'What I'm getting at is that if you shy away from me every time I come near you it's bound to appear odd.'

'I wasn't aware that I did,' she muttered.

'You do. Mortifyingly often. Why?'

Because if I don't, thought Eliza, you might discover that, far from being repulsive, Giles Randolph, you're everything in life I've ever wanted. But I'll keep my secret, even if it kills me.

'I promise I won't shy away in public, then,' she said at last.

'Show me.'

'We're not in public now!' Eliza eyed him with such suspicion that Giles laughed shortly.

'Don't look like that, Eliza. All I had in mind was a kiss!'

'Oh, all right,' she said grudgingly. She held up her mouth, closed her eyes and waited. When nothing happened she opened them again questioningly to find Giles regarding her with amusement.

'You really know how to switch a man off,' he said, shaking his head. He jumped to his feet. 'Come on, I'll drive you home.'

Eliza, thoroughly deflated, sat in silence for most of the drive back to Pennington.

'Will you come up for coffee?' she asked when they arrived.

Giles helped her out of the car, his eyes searching. 'Would you like me to?'

'Yes,' said Eliza, wishing now that she'd stayed at Tithe Barn. She ran up the stairs ahead of Giles, suddenly worried that he'd read more into the invitation than she intended. Inside her flat his presence was so overpowering that she begged him to sit down, play some music, switch on the television. Anything rather than watch her in silence. He shook his head, leaning at the door of her tiny kitchen, his eyes never leaving her face. Cursing herself for sudden, absurd shyness, she maintained a flow of inconsequential chatter which Giles silenced very effectively at last by taking the coffee-tray from her, dumping it on a table and pulling her into his arms.

'For pity's sake shut up, Eliza!' He swung her off her feet and she clutched at him, her mouth opening with a ragged sigh as he kissed her. The kiss grew fierce as he sat down with her on the sofa, holding her so tightly she couldn't move. Not that she had the least desire to. This, if Giles only knew, was what she wanted more than anything else in the world. She locked her hands behind his taut neck, her fingers caressing the crisp gold hair at his nape as she returned his kisses with abandon, her pulse racing and her blood fizzing in her veins like champagne. Her lips parted gladly to his tongue, her breasts hardening to the caress of his expert, coaxing hands and she exulted as the stirring hardness beneath her thighs told her very plainly how much he wanted her.

Giles raised his head at last and stared down at her, breathing hard, his eyes glittering darkly as he held her prisoner against his chest, which heaved convulsively against her breasts as he fought for control. For a long, tense interval there was no sound in the room other than their breathing, until at last, unable to bear the silence any longer, Eliza managed a shaky smile and said, 'Would you like some coffee now?'

Giles released her slowly, a wry curve to the lips that had just been kissing her senseless. 'No, Eliza. I'd much rather take you to bed and make love to you all night, as must be perfectly obvious. But I'll settle for coffee if I must.'

Eliza swayed slightly as she got to her feet, her head still reeling from his assault on her senses. 'Just as well,' she said, trying for lightness. 'I don't think my single bed could cope with someone like you, Giles.'

His smile mocked her. 'Its size must restrict your love-life, Eliza.'

'Not in the least,' she said with perfect truth, then handed him a cup with a hand so unsteady half the coffee spilled into the saucer. 'I'll pour you another,' she said hastily, but Giles took it from her and dumped it on the tray again.

'To hell with the coffee,' he said harshly, and pulled her down beside him again.

'Giles——' she began in fright, but he shook his head impatiently, seizing her hand.

'I want to explain, Eliza.'

'Explain a goodnight kiss?'

He smiled sardonically. 'Is that all it was?'

'No,' she admitted with a sigh.

'You know perfectly well that what happened just now should have led us straight to bed.'

Since such an incident was totally outside her experience Eliza said nothing, suppressing a shiver at the mere thought of it.

'Believe me, it was bloody difficult to slam on the brakes!' He looked down at her hand, smoothing his thumb over the back of it in a caress which, in her present state of hormonal unrest, made it difficult for Eliza to sit still. 'You haven't asked me why I stopped.'

'Perhaps you thought I might take our engagement seriously,' she said demurely, her eyes glittering. 'I assumed the prospect brought you back to earth with a bump.'

'You assumed wrong. I stopped,' he said very deliberately, holding her eyes with his, 'because it suddenly occurred to me that if I gave in to the demands of my much tried libido, you'd think I was demanding payment for this.' He held up her hand so that the glittering stones in the ring caught the light. 'Which I won't. I fabricated the story, so it's *mea culpa*. You were presented with the engagement as a *fait accompli* whether you liked it or not. But apart from that, something you once said hit me like a missile before I reached the point of no return.'

Eliza pushed back her hair, frowning. 'What was that?'

'You said you never make love with a man unless you really want to. And I could never have been sure that you did want to, or whether you felt obliged, if I'd ridden roughshod and taken you off to bed.'

Couldn't he *tell* she wanted to? she thought irritably. Men, even men with as much experience of women as Giles, could be extraordinarily dense on occasion. 'Oh, well,' she said prosaically, 'it's all academic now, anyway, and no harm done.'

'Speak for yourself,' said Giles bitterly, and got to his feet. 'When do I see you again? Now we're engaged, I trust you realise you're landed with my company now and then, if only to keep up appearances.'

'No hardship,' she assured him, deliberately casual to disguise such a literal truth. 'Pity it's so far for you to travel.'

'A small price to pay for the privilege!' He took out a diary, frowning. 'As it happens, I can't see you until Friday. I'm pretty much tied up until then.'

Eliza was rather glad of the respite. After a weekend of such unrelenting emotional mayhem it was a relief to get down to work, despite a trying tendency on the part of her colleagues to harp on the subject of matrimony once she'd displayed the ring, as Giles had instructed. Fending off questions about a wedding date was relatively easy, due to her parents' absence. And by the time they returned from New Zealand the whole thing would probably be over. Her work on Combe Farm would have reached the point of no return. Paul and Gemma could be safely engaged, or equally safely have parted. Either way Giles would be let off the hook, this charade of an engagement could die a decent death and Eliza Markham's life could return to normal, a prospect she found depressingly unappealing.

During the week Eliza discovered that one of the reasons for maintaining the pretence would soon cease to exist. She had a stroke of luck in hearing about an exquisite staircase crying out for rescue from a building due for demolition. She snaffled it instantly for Combe Farm, the coup winning her enormous respect from Paul Wright, who promptly approved all her estimates and designs and told her to go ahead at full steam.

Paul the businessman, she found to her relief, was a different cup of tea from the man who'd brought Gemma to lunch. During their telephone conversations he treated Eliza with the respect due one professional from another. Then one day his tone changed before he rang off, standing the hair up on the back of her neck.

'I've been thinking. You and I should get to know each other better, one way and another, Liza. Giles is often away, so is Gem. When their trips coincide why not come up to town for an evening with me some time?'

Eliza, appalled, made polite non-committal noises, and rang off before she said something rash.

The days rushed by, accelerated by her workload, some of them so protracted in Eliza's eagerness to get the Combe Farm project over and done with as quickly as possible that her evenings were short, some of them rounded off, to Eliza's pleased surprise, by a phone call from Giles just before bedtime.

'Just checking you're not carousing with some other man while my back's turned,' he said the first time.

'Unless he sells curtains or furniture, or cans of paint, I haven't got time, far less inclination,' she assured him, yawning.

'Good. Talking of other men, have you heard from Lawrence?'

Eliza told him she most certainly had, relating the incident with relish. Lawrence had turned up on her doorstep on her first evening at home, laden with flowers and verbose with apologies. Eliza refused to let him across her threshold and told him exactly what he could do with the flowers.

'He was terribly wounded,' she told Giles.

'If he persists he will be—by contact with my fist!'

'No need. When I flashed the ring he was defeated, horse, foot and guns!'

'I thought it would come in handy.' He paused. 'You haven't forgotten I'm coming over on Friday evening?'

Eliza, who had trouble in thinking about anything else, assured him lightly she hadn't, and went on to tell him about Paul's suggestion.

Giles was silent for a moment, then said grimly, 'Eliza, if I hadn't had the foresight to think up this engagement I'm sure Paul would ditch Gemma like a shot and come chasing after you.'

Eliza sighed. 'I hate to say it, but I'm beginning to think you're right. I owe you, Giles.'

'So you do. I'll think of some way you can repay me.'

Far from forgetting her evening with Giles, Eliza was looking forward to it so much that she was quite dismayed when Charmian suggested she bring Giles along to the Lucas household first for a drink.

'We won't keep you long, dear, just half an hour before you go out to paint the town red. I'm dying to meet him.'

Giles, to her surprise, was all for the idea, assuring her he was quite happy to act the part of doting fiancé.

'This is all getting a bit out of hand,' she said despairingly. 'I've had Mother on the line from Auckland, driving Dad insane with the cost of the phone call while she went on about cakes and bridesmaids and guest-lists. I felt like a criminal, Giles!'

'Don't worry. I'll divert all the flak when the time comes, I promise.'

'You bet your boots you will!'

Charmian was greatly amused to find Eliza had splashed out on another dress.

'What happened to the other one? After all the money you paid for it I was sure you'd wear it again tonight.'

'The dress and I got very wet last Saturday. It diminished, I didn't,' fibbed Eliza in defence of her latest purchase, which was the exact shade of the emerald in the ring, a coincidence which failed to escape her teasing employer's eye.

Eliza finished work on the stroke of five-thirty that evening, determined to lavish so much care and attention on her appearance that Giles would be bowled over by the result. She was so intent on her task that Giles arrived before she'd finished dressing. Eliza pulled on a kimono before opening the door, then shaded her eyes, mock-dazzled at the sight of him in festive cobalt silk waistcoat and tie and magnificent dark suit, his arms filled with crimson roses.

'Gosh, Giles, you look terrific! But you're early.'

'No, I'm on time. You're late.' He tossed the flowers on a table, seized her in his arms and planted a hard, swift kiss on her parted mouth before standing back to smile down at her. 'How's my pretend betrothed?'

'Well, but overworked.'

'Good. Keeps you out of mischief.' He handed her the flowers with a bow. 'For you.'

Eliza inhaled their scent with pleasure, filled a pottery jug with water and began arranging the flowers on the small table between the windows while Giles asked for her current news.

'Nothing new since I spoke to you last night—unless you count the new dress I bought today.'

Giles stood with arms folded, watching her. 'Will I approve of this one?'

'I hope so. No distinguishing marks on view, I promise.'

He reached out and took her by the shoulders, turning her towards him. 'Eliza, I lie awake at night thinking of your famous birthmark.'

'Because Paul's seen it and you haven't?'

'Partly.'

Eliza looked up at him, smiling a little. 'Pity to give you insomnia. But it's nothing very remarkable.' Holding his eyes, she slid the kimono from her shoulders, her colour mounting as Giles gazed at the tiny black mark standing out in relief between the fullness of curves only partly concealed by her grey satin camisole.

'Are you satisfied now?' she asked, not looking at him as she pulled the kimono back into place.

Giles let out a deep breath. 'As a cure for insomnia, Eliza, that was a dismal failure.'

'You're hard to please!'

'Not at all,' he said softly, and took her hands. 'You could please me very easily indeed.'

'We're late,' said Eliza hastily. 'I'd better finish dressing.'

Giles's mocking laugh followed her as she escaped to her bedroom, but his eyes gleamed with admiration when she reappeared with hair smooth, lipstick back in place, the neckline of the brief, sleeveless dress high enough to win instant approval.

'You look ravishing!'

'So do you,' Eliza assured him as they went down to his car. 'Charmian will be *most* impressed.'

Graeme and Charmian Lucas lived in one of the tall narrow houses surrounding a tree-lined square on the outskirts of town. Now their children were grown up, the house served as a showcase these days for Charmian's talents, and was used regularly to entertain prospective clients and business contacts. As Giles parked the car under chestnut trees ablaze with pink candles, Eliza eyed the house with her usual pleasure.

'I love this place.'

'You prefer life in a town?'

'Not specially. I love the country, too. But this is where I ply my trade.' Before Eliza could reach for the brass lion-head knocker the door opened and

Charmian stood there, elegant as always, her smile mischievous as Eliza introduced Giles.

'Congratulations! I've been longing to meet you. Eliza tried to tell me you were just her brother's friend, but I knew all along there was more to it than that!'

'It was true enough, Mrs Lucas,' said Giles, smiling, his arm round Eliza's shoulders. 'But now I've persuaded her into a closer relationship. I'm a very lucky man.'

Charmian kissed Eliza's cheek warmly. 'I think you're a lucky lady, too. Oh, by the way, just one or two people here, dear,' she said and led them along the hall to a drawing-room crowded, to Eliza's consternation, with everyone connected with the firm.

Eliza stiffened, not daring to look at Giles as his arm tightened round her waist. Graeme Lucas handed them glasses of champagne while everyone crowded round, showering the surprised pair not only with good wishes, to Eliza's horror, but with gift-wrapped packages the donors insisted must be unwrapped at once.

'With your parents on the other side of the world, pet,' said Graeme affectionately, 'Charmian couldn't rest until she'd organised a little party for you.'

'It's extraordinarily kind of you,' said Giles, his fingers pinching Eliza hard as he smiled down at her in a way which brought a sigh from every female in the room. 'We deeply appreciate it, don't we, darling?'

'You really shouldn't have,' said Eliza with desperate sincerity. 'I didn't expect——'

'Nonsense,' said Charmian. 'I was longing to meet your Giles anyway.' She gave him a roguish look. 'Nor am I disappointed.'

'I envy Eliza such a charming boss,' he returned suavely, with a smile which delighted Charmian but won him a kindling backward look from Eliza as she was borne away to unwrap presents.

It was more than an hour before she could detach Giles, who was enjoying himself so much that she was irritable by the time they drove away from the house in Prince's Square.

'I'm glad you think it's funny!' she snapped. 'You won't be working there after—afterwards.'

Giles was infuriatingly unrepentant. 'I must admit that tonight came as a surprise. It was one contingency I hadn't allowed for.'

'You mean you hadn't thought of *everything*?' she said crossly. 'I could have sunk through the floor when the cleaning lady gave us that little Spode bowl. Even with a chip it's still quite valuable.'

'Very thoughtful,' agreed Giles, unruffled. 'I'm sure she'll be sympathetic if you hand it back.'

'Maybe I won't hand it back!' Eliza slanted her eyes at him. 'I might just keep everything for next time.'

His brows flew together. 'Next time?'

'Yes. I'll probably get engaged for real some time. Most girls do, you know.'

'Frankly, it seems extraordinary to me that you haven't been snapped up long ago.'

'Gemma hasn't either, remember!'

'That's different. For some reason it's hard to associate Gemma with children and domesticity.'

'I thought you found her very appealing once upon a time.'

Giles frowned blankly. 'Why do you say that? *You* were the one who appealed, Eliza. I thought I made that blindingly obvious the day of the wedding.'

'Don't bring that up again!'

'Sorry.' He breathed in deeply. 'Go on. You were talking about Gemma—as usual.'

'Sorry to keep on, but Giles, I just can't see why she's so set on Paul. One or two of his ideas for his bedroom stood my hair on end—a four-poster with a mirror lining the tester, would you believe?'

Giles gave an exclamation of distaste, then put a hand on her knee. 'Forget about Paul tonight, Eliza. Let's just enjoy the evening like any normal newly engaged couple. Though in one way I suppose he did me a favour.'

'How?'

He turned her face up to his. 'If he hadn't insisted I turn up at his party that night, you and I might never have met up again.'

She laughed unsteadily. 'Think of the trouble you'd have been saved if we hadn't.'

He bent his head and kissed her, his mouth lingering on hers with a pleasure he made no attempt to hide. He raised his head at last, his eyes glittering as they met the slumbrous look in hers. 'The compensations more than make up for it, Eliza.' He touched a finger to her cheek, then got out of the car. 'Come on. Let's eat. I'm starving.'

CHAPTER ELEVEN

BY THE end of a capricious, showery June Eliza had grown so used to her make-believe engagement that it had ceased, ominously, to feel like a charade at all. She saw Giles regularly once or twice a week, hung his curtains for him at Tithe Barn after all—to Charmian's amusement—and grew so used to wearing the beautiful emerald ring that she closed her mind to the time when, inevitably, she'd have to hand it back.

Work on Combe Farm was going well, to the point where she had time to spare from it for other commissions. And as time went by she chafed secretly at the restraint Giles placed on their relationship. He took care, for the most part, to indulge in no more than a kiss or two when they were together. Now and again the tension between them would tauten unbearably and he would seize her in his arms and kiss her until she felt she would explode, or go mad, if he didn't take her to bed. But he never did. And she knew why, she thought with bitterness. Giles kept an iron rein on his impulses for the simple reason that her name was Markham. His respect for her parents and allegiance to her brother were powerful impediments to a love affair with their Eliza. Giles firmly believed her family would expect marriage, and he'd made his views on that so plain, the spectre of future heartbreak would have haunted her constantly if she'd let it.

Soon, she thought with gloom, her parents would be home. And then life would get complicated. Gemma was already growing more and more persistent about her sister's wedding plans, with never a hint of any change in her own relationship with Paul.

Things came to a head after a lonely, aimless weekend without Giles, who was away on a trip to the Continent. Gemma was on a fashion shoot in Ireland, and Eliza was so tired of her own company by Monday morning that she was glad of a working day which was so busy that she was totally unprepared for the balloon that went up at the end of it. But it was a balloon of a very different colour from the one Eliza had dreaded for so long.

She was tired after an afternoon spent in baking hot temperatures at the house of a client who wanted her attic converted into bedrooms. The heat in the small rooms had been intense, the lady indecisive, and Eliza was thoroughly out of sorts by the time she got home to her flat, which was like an oven after being closed up all day in the summer heat. As the final straw, when the phone rang the moment she was through the door the call was from Gemma, not Giles as she'd hoped.

'Guess what? When I got back this afternoon, Paul was waiting at the airport.' Gemma laughed, sounding wildly excited. 'He finally got round to proposing, Liza!'

Eliza stared blindly at the ring on her finger. 'That—that's wonderful, love, I'm so happy for you. I know how much you wanted——'

'Which only goes to show what an imbecile I am,' declared Gemma, utterly confounding her sister.

'*What*?'

'To be honest, I began to have doubts about Paul after the day we spent with you and Giles. Seeing you two together, so utterly right for each other, made me realise Paul was all wrong—for me, anyway.'

Eliza sat down with a thump. 'Gem, hang on a minute. Are you saying that Paul proposed and you *refused*?'

'Yes. Bit of a laugh, really, isn't it?' Gemma paused. 'Liza, will you scream if I say there's someone else?'

Eliza breathed in deeply. 'Provided my help isn't required to keep him up to scratch, sister dear, I'll try not to.'

'You *are* fed up with me.'

'Just a bit.'

'Don't you want to know who the man is?'

'Do I know him?'

'Oh, yes.' Gemma gave a choked little laugh. 'Actually, it's Tom.'

'Tom?' repeated Eliza blankly. 'Wait a minute, Gem. Do you mean Tom Metcalfe?'

'Yes. Fancy a double wedding? It'll be much cheaper for Dad!'

Eliza went to bed that night in a state of shock. Gemma had lived for the past five years in a Victorian house in Clapham, inherited by Tom Metcalfe from his grandparents. At first she'd shared the top-floor flat with another girl, while Tom lived alone in the basement and let the garden apartment to a young couple. Currently Gemma lived alone in her flat and Tom alone in the rest of the house. Lanky, humorous, with light, shrewd eyes, sandy hair, and a steady career in banking, he was so much the antithesis of any other man in Gemma's adult life that Eliza still couldn't visualise them as a pair.

She liked Tom. Over the years she'd met him often. Gemma invited him to parties, and looked on him as a steady and valued friend. And plenty of ladies popped in and out of Tom's place, according to Gemma. One had even lived there with him for a while. But it seemed that all these years he'd been biding his time, waiting for Gemma to come to her senses. And the moment Paul had asked her to marry him, she had. Suddenly, as if a light had been switched on in her brain, Gemma had realised the only man in the world she could face marriage with was Tom.

'We've shared the same house for years anyway,' she'd told Eliza earlier. 'I've moved downstairs, that's all.'

'You've *moved*?'

'Oh, yes. I'm speaking from Tom's place now. When I came down to tell him Paul was history Tom simply locked the door and said I could stay here until I promised to marry him instead, which took about two seconds. And after that there seemed no point in leaving. We'll get married as soon as Mother and Dad get back.' Gemma cleared her throat. 'Liza.'

'Yes?'

'Have you told Giles? About the lies I told you at the wedding?' She sighed audibly. 'I was like a cat on hot bricks the day we had lunch.'

'I told him the moment I knew. It seemed only fair.'

'You mean he knew that day and didn't throw it in my face?'

'That's right.'

Gemma whistled. 'I never thought you'd find a man good enough for you, Liza, but I was wrong. We were both so mad over Giles at one time. I never realised you still were, you know. Funny how things turned out.'

'Utterly hilarious! Now put Tom on so I can congratulate him.'

Eliza lay wide-eyed and wakeful for most of the night after Gemma's bombshell, facing the fact that her time as Giles's fiancée was over. She would give him the news in person the moment he returned, hand back the ring and absolve him of further responsibility. With Gemma about to marry Tom, and the work on Combe Farm too far advanced for Paul to cancel it out of sheer spite, the mock engagement could die as quick and merciful a death as possible.

The day Giles was due back she drove to Little Rencombe on an evening bright and warm with high summer, the sunshine a painful contrast with the gloom in her heart. She let herself into the house with the key Giles had once given her, then went to let Poppy out for a long walk to pass the time. When Eliza trudged back, hot and untidy with the panting dog at her heels, Giles was pacing up and down beside her car, looking tired and irritable, and by no means brimming over with welcome at the sight of her.

'Where the hell have you been?' he demanded, hauling her into the house. 'I went straight from the airport to your place but you weren't there.'

'How did I know you intended that?' she snapped. 'I drove over here because I needed to see you urgently.'

Giles stopped dead. 'What's wrong?'

'I just thought you'd like to know Gemma's getting married.' Eliza smiled brightly and held out the ring. 'So there's no need for this any more.'

Giles stared at the ring blankly for a moment then turned on his heel. 'I need a drink.'

'So do I. Brandy.'

He swung round to look at her in surprise. 'Brandy?'

'Yes,' she said defiantly.

Eyebrows raised he poured a small measure of brandy into a glass, then a larger tot of whisky into another, splashed soda into both then handed a glass to her with a slight, ceremonious bow.

'To Gemma, then.'

'To Gemma,' echoed Eliza, and downed her brandy in a rash gulp which brought on a spasm of coughing and spluttering.

Giles rescued the glass, patted her back, brought her a glass of water and after a while, when all was quiet again, he led her to a sofa and sat down beside her. 'Sip it next time,' he advised.

'So when are Gemma and Paul tying the knot?' he asked after several seconds spent staring into his drink.

'Oh, didn't I say? She's not marrying Paul.'

'*What*!' Giles turned Eliza to face him with an un-gentle hand, his eyes blazing. 'Are you serious?'

Eliza explained Gemma's change of heart as suc-cinctly as she could in the face of Giles's wrath.

'I don't think it was a *change* of heart, exactly, Giles,' she said by way of extenuation. 'I mean, she's known Tom for years.'

'There should be a government warning against a relationship with the Markham twins,' said Giles murderously. 'It's bloody dangerous.'

Eliza jumped to her feet, her eyes flashing. 'Not for you. Not any more.' She thrust the ring at him. 'I don't need this now.'

Giles hurled it across the room in rage. 'You seem to have missed a point here. Paul is now on the loose good and proper; you're the spitting image of the lady who jilted him. And I'm convinced it's you he's really lusted after ever since that blasted party of his. Not Gemma.'

'I can take care of myself,' she said, secretly very shaken by one aspect of the situation which hadn't occurred to her.

'Don't talk such rot.'

She glared at him, incensed. 'It's true!'

'Oh, no, it's not, as I know, better than anyone, Eliza.' Giles got to his feet, looking very intimidating as he loomed over her. 'On two separate occasions you've found it very difficult to take care of yourself. The first time I just happened to be on hand to come to your rescue and the second time I made bloody sure I was. But if Paul hears we've split up and comes gunning for you some day when I'm not around, I don't fancy your chances a third time.'

Eliza's mouth set stubbornly. 'As you so often tell me, I'm no longer ten years old. I'm perfectly able to cope, even if anything so unlikely were to happen.'

'Talk sense, Eliza! Paul's a cocky lad drunk with his own success and used to women falling at his feet. Half Gemma's attraction for him was the fact that she's a well-known model, someone to add to his image. But she rejected him. Picture the mood he's in right now. If he finds out you're fancy-free——' Giles eyed her scathingly. 'I leave the rest to your imagination.'

'Even if he did come raping and pillaging,' said Eliza defiantly, 'I'm a match for someone Paul's size.'

He laughed in derision. 'If Paul—or any man—has rape on his mind, Eliza, physique doesn't enter into it. You wouldn't stand a chance.'

'I don't believe that!'

They stood glaring at each other in deadlock, then Giles clicked his fingers at Poppy and shut her in the kitchen. He strolled back towards Eliza, his face expressionless as he discarded his jacket and took off his tie.

'I'd better go,' she said, backing away uneasily.

'Not before we've conducted a little experiment.' And before she had any inkling of his intention he tossed her down on the Bokhara rug she'd chosen for him, parted her legs and knelt between them, keeping her captive so effortlessly she panicked.

'Let me up, you maniac!' she screeched, arms and legs flailing in vain. 'What do you think you're *doing*?'

'I am demonstrating,' he panted, holding her shoulders flat on the floor, 'how vulnerable you would be.'

She fought like a tigress to avoid his descending mouth, but he laughed and held her still, his eyes glittering with a light which scared her witless.

'No—please!' She pushed at him in panic.

'Not this time, sweetheart! You owe me this——'

'*No*—you don't understand——'

Giles stifled her protests with his mouth, then raised his head a fraction to stare into her dilated eyes. 'Ah, but I do! Now my services are no longer required you intend to waltz through that door and leave me flat again, just as you did before. Well this time, little teaser, I'm not letting you escape so easily!'

Hot, salty tears slid from the corners of her eyes, and she twisted her head away. 'I didn't want to escape last time,' she muttered thickly, and felt his body tense above hers.

'What did you say?'

'You heard me. I wanted you as much as you seemed to want me.' She turned her head to look straight up into his eyes as he hung over her. 'I led you on that day to punish you, true enough. But not for the reason you think. It wasn't because you'd been with Gemma, as she said. I was jealous because I wanted it to be *me*. To this day I don't know where I found the strength to push you away. I wanted you to make love to me more than anything in the world.'

Giles stared at her incredulously, then leapt up, bending to yank her to her feet. He took her elbows in a bruising grip, his eyes burning into hers. 'Why didn't you tell me this before?'

She quailed before the look in Giles's eyes as his grip tightened. 'Because until not so long ago I thought you'd tried to seduce Gemma, and I couldn't forgive you for preferring her to me. Then, when I told you——' She drew in a quivering breath. 'You couldn't forgive me for believing her.'

He let her go so suddenly that she stumbled. 'Gemma has no idea of the trouble she caused, does she? I've lain awake many a long night, wondering what the hell I'd done to deserve the treatment you two dished out to me that day. First Gemma, with her embarrassing overtures, which I rejected pretty cruelly, I admit. Then minutes later I thought I was dreaming when you drifted up to me, invitation in every line of you. One look, one touch of your hand, and I wanted you so much I lost my head completely.

Extraordinary, really. You two are so much alike, yet Gemma's always left me cold. While you can set me on fire just by being in the same room.' He frowned as he saw a tear roll down her cheeks.

'Why are you crying?'

'Why do you think?' she said angrily, scrubbing at her eyes.

'Are you unhappy?'

She laughed scornfully. 'Why on earth should I be unhappy?'

'I don't know. But I'm going to find out.' Giles cupped her shoulders in his hands. 'Tell me what's wrong, Eliza.' His eyes bored into hers like laser beams. 'Is it possible you don't *want* our engagement to end!'

Eliza stared at him with wet eyes. 'Do you?'

He muttered something unintelligible, then pulled her into his arms and kissed her until neither could breathe. Eliza's knees gave way, but when Giles would have picked her up she tugged hard on his arms instead to bring him down with her to the rug again. She stretched against his hard, muscular body, locking her hands behind his head as he kissed her mouth, her eyes, her earlobes, the taut line of her throat. Slowly he began to unfasten her shirt, his mouth still on hers. Her lips parted, inviting the caress of his tongue, her back arching as he slid the shirt from her shoulders. He raised his head to look down at her for a long, silent moment, then bent to lay his mouth on the birthmark between her breasts.

Giles looked up to meet her heavy, brilliant eyes. 'Do you know how much I've wanted to do that?'

'I hoped,' she whispered.

'You said you were in love with me once, Eliza. Are you still?'

She stared into his dilating eyes. 'No more words, Giles. Can't you just make love to me?'

'I'd like a little encouragement first.'

She flushed, blinking. 'I thought I'd given you rather a lot already.'

'I want the verbal kind,' he said inexorably.

She smiled sleepily. 'It's all right, Giles. I won't expect a wedding ring, I promise.'

Giles gave a stifled exclamation, then kissed her until her head was reeling, tearing his mouth away at last to kiss her breasts, his lips teasing and coaxing, his teeth grazing the nipples in such delicate torture that she gasped his name in frantic supplication. And suddenly they were straining together in a feverish tangle of seeking hands and mouths, of clothing discarded by one or the other in desperate haste until they lay together motionless as their bodies came into complete naked contact for the first time. Giles hung over her, his eyes alight with a question Eliza answered without words, her hands drumming a tattoo of demand on his back, her entire body throbbing with delight in response to his coaxing, clever hands. She heard herself pleading, and Giles's breathless laugh, warm against her parted mouth. Then her eyes widened, her breath catching in her throat as their bodies came together in a moment of such perfection that tears slid down her cheeks, salt against his mouth.

Giles tensed. 'I hurt you?'

'No.' She smiled through her tears into his taut face, and moved against him delicately, thrusting her hips against his in an invitation he accepted with controlled, subtle skill at first until his desire outrode his restraint and he surrendered to his own urgency, taking her with him at rhythmic speed towards the fulfilment which engulfed them both, then died away slowly, leaving an exquisite lassitude in its wake.

It was a long time before Giles raised his head to look down into her flushed face.

'Are you convinced?' he enquired huskily.

She looked up at him, dazed. 'Of what?'

'That you wouldn't have stood a chance against Paul.'

'No.'

'*No*!'

'You're bigger than he is.'

'I told you that's got nothing to do with it.' Giles smoothed the hair back from her damp forehead.

'Besides...'

'Besides what?'

Eliza looked away, her colour deepening.

Giles put a hand under her chin, forcing her to meet his eyes. 'Besides what?'

Eliza glared at him. 'Do I have to spell it out? With you it's—different. I just can't imagine letting Paul near enough for—for any of that to be possible. What Gemma ever saw in him beats me.'

'Power, money, perhaps.'

She smiled. 'Tom's a bit lacking in both, yet the moment he proposed Gemma accepted like a shot and promptly moved in with him.'

'Mysterious lot, you females.' Giles held her closer. 'Eliza.'

'Yes.'

'I've got a confession to make, too.'

She groaned. 'Not you as well, Giles! I don't want to hear it.'

'Yes, you do.' He kissed her gently, then kissed her again, not nearly so gently. 'Where was I?' he said after a while.

Eliza shifted a little. 'I'd better get dressed——'

He held her fast. 'No. Never interrupt a man when he's confessing. To start with I want you to know how much I love you.'

Colour surged into her face then receded, leaving her ivory-pale beneath her tan. 'Are—are you serious?'

'Deadly serious. Is it so hard to believe, Eliza?'

She nodded violently. 'You said you *wanted* me, which is a very different thing. I thought the engagement was just a way of putting Paul off without losing him as a business contact.'

'The first bit's right, but the rest of it was such a flimsy excuse I'm amazed you believed it. I don't care a toss for Paul and his contacts, nor did I ever think him right for Gemma. But she was none of my business. It was when he started leching after you that I saw red.' Giles secured her hands efficiently. 'Just so you don't hit me.'

'Why should I hit you?' she demanded suspiciously.

'Because I've got a bit more to confess! You may as well know that it was my idea to get you to do up Tithe Barn. Nothing to do with Rob. It seemed like a foolproof way to see you regularly. To get you used to having me around. Because I took one look at you that night at Paul's party and realised why marriage to Marina, or anyone other than you, had always been out of the question.'

Eliza stared at him narrowly. 'You swore it was marriage itself that scared you stiff.'

'A little ignoble retaliation on my part, darling.' He smiled. 'You are not an easy lady to court, Eliza Markham. You keep hurling unjust accusations at me. But when I went to see Paul to clear up our latest little misunderstanding I told him the literal truth. That you were mine. Then I drove straight down to you to tell you the same thing. And there you were, all dressed up like a Christmas tree for another man. I could have murdered you.' His eyes hardened. 'I'm only human, Eliza. I was off my head with jealousy. So I cooked up our little charade to keep you tethered, determined to make you admit you loved me before I proposed for real.'

'Men are so unbelievably *dense*,' said Eliza pityingly. 'And blind. I've been in love with you since I was ten years old. At a rough guess I suppose I'll go on loving you—heaven knows why—for the rest of my life.'

Giles breathed in sharply then kissed her hard, hugging her until her ribs protested. 'Why couldn't you give me a sign, you witch?'

'How was I to know you wanted one?' she said crossly, and pushed him away. 'And while we're making confessions I suppose you'd better hear the real reason why the demonstration you just made was pointless.'

Giles face drained of expression. 'Why was it pointless?'

'As a demonstration of how easy it is to overcome a woman it was a complete washout. Surely you noticed there wasn't any resistance?' Her eyes danced, igniting a flame in his.

'Little devil!' he muttered against her mouth.

'Besides, you know you mow most women down just with a smile!'

'Since I found you again there haven't been any women. Only you.'

'I'm happy to hear it. I hate the thought of other women trespassing in that kitchen.'

'It's not my kitchen they're interested in!'

Eliza shot up with a shriek of indignation. 'You mean they spend all their time in bed?'

'No.' Giles pulled her back down again. 'I mean that no other women, other than my wonderful Mrs Treasure, have ever set foot in the place. I moved in only a week or two before I ran into you that night, remember, after which my interest in other members of your sex died a sudden death. My house is so much yours in every way, Eliza, I'll sell the place if you won't live here with me.'

She wreathed her arms round his neck. 'I'll move in tomorrow.'

He kissed her hard. 'I only wish I could take you up on that.'

'Why can't you? Gemma's moved in with Tom.'

'But you and Gemma, as you keep telling me, are two very separate people,' Giles reminded her swiftly. 'Having got this far, I think I can manage on my own—just—until we're married.'

She pursed her lips. 'I just can't get used to the fact that marriage doesn't scare you to death.' She frowned. 'But it would be a bit far for me to drive to Pennington every day, Giles.'

'Then don't,' he said promptly. 'What's to stop you coming in with me instead? Lots of interior designers work in conjunction with architects. We'd make the perfect team—in every way.'

She considered the idea thoughtfully. 'Are you sure you want that? We'd be together rather a lot.'

'I don't consider that a problem. I hope you don't either,' he added menacingly.

'No. No problem at all.' She smiled at him seraphically. 'But I expect full pay when I take time off to have babies.'

Giles crushed her close, kissing her in a way which put an end to conversation for some time, until at last Eliza pushed him away as her stomach gave a very unromantic rumble.

'I haven't had anything to eat today, Giles. I'm starving!'

He pulled her up, laughing. 'Our recent occupation does rather tend to stimulate the appetite.'

She dressed hastily, not looking at him. 'You'd know a lot more about that than me.'

He drew her into his arms. 'Eliza, whatever my past has been—and it hasn't been anything like as hectic as you imagine—my future belongs to you, and you alone.'

She leaned back against his linked hands, meeting his eyes candidly. 'Which is only fair, because you've been a terrible impediment to my love-life in the past. You've come between me and every man I've ever met. I kept comparing them all with you. And they lost every time.'

Giles locked his arms round her and kissed her hard, eventually picking her up to sit down with her on his lap, forgetting about food as he told her a great many deeply gratifying things.

'What are you thinking about?' he asked after a while. 'Your eyes are full of dreams.'

She gave him an abstracted smile. 'Actually, I was just thinking I'd like to take the table over there with the velvet cloth up to the bedroom to go with the padded stool Charmian gave us——'

'*What*?' Giles held her away. 'And here was I, thinking you were ravished by the proximity of my body!'

'I was, I was! But thoughts of that nature led me to thoughts of your bedroom—a perfectly logical progression. And believe me, your bedroom will have to perk up a lot if I'm going to sleep there.'

'Make what changes you like—short of miles of blue silk,' he assured her, then tried to pull her back as she slid off his lap to grovel on the floor. 'What are you doing *now*?'

'Looking for my ring,' she said, pouncing on it. She smiled at him as she handed it over. 'You can put it on for me, with an appropriate word now it's for real.'

Giles slid it on her finger, then raised her hand to his lips, looking at her over it. 'With this ring I thee wed, with my body I thee worship—will that do?'

She blinked hard. 'I—I think that's meant for a different ring.'

'Same sentiments, Eliza, now and always.' He took her in his arms and kissed her with a commitment which thrilled her as much as the passion of his earlier lovemaking.

'I was so unhappy when I came here this afternoon,' she confessed later, when they were walking through the woods with Poppy.

'And now?'

She turned to look at him, her eyes lambent with love in the evening sunlight. 'Now I'm the happiest creature alive.'

His hand crushed hers. 'Let's go out and celebrate——'

'Like this?' She laughed, waving a hand at her denim skirt and crumpled shirt. 'I've got a better idea. Let's stay *in* and celebrate. We'll eat whatever goodies Mrs Treasure has left for you, and then——' She paused, deliberately tantalising.

'And then,' said Giles, resigned, 'I suppose you're going to leave me and drive home.'

'Well, no,' she said, as they went back into the house. 'I thought I might stay the night, since it's a special occasion. I'll drive back at the crack of dawn.'

Giles lifted her by the elbows and perched her on the kitchen table, his hands loosely clasped behind her back. 'Would it offend your sensibilities to ask which bed you intend sleeping in?'

'Not at all. Yours,' she assured him. 'Because I'm hoping to seduce you into granting a rather tricky request.'

Giles kissed her, laughing against her parted mouth. 'I'll look forward to that! Not that you need wait, Eliza. Ask away right now. If it's within my power to give, you shall have anything your heart desires, I promise.'

She returned the kiss with interest. 'I think I'd better keep to my plan, just the same. My request requires you in a desperately weakened state.'

'Tell me now!' he ordered sternly.

'Oh, all right.' Eliza took in a deep breath. 'Gemma suggested we have a double wedding to save Dad expense. Could you possibly endure that?'

Giles gave a shout of laughter. 'I suppose I could. What happens if I marry the wrong girl?'

'No chance. I'll have my dress cut low enough to show my beauty spot.'

'You will not!' Giles bent his head to kiss the famous birthmark. 'Besides, you can't fool me. You and Gemma may be twins, but to me, my darling Eliza, *you* are one of a kind. Unique.'

She smiled jubilantly. 'Likewise, Mr Randolph. In fact I've loved only one other male so desperately in my entire life.'

'Who?' he demanded wrathfully.

'Lucky, my pony, of course!'

'Witch!' He shook her slightly. 'I'm not joking, either. You cast a spell over me the minute I found you again at Paul's party, even with all the curls and cleavage.' He leered at her outrageously. 'On second thoughts, maybe because of the cleavage.'

She sniffed. 'Don't be vulgar! Anyway, if I wave my wand *will* you say yes to a double wedding?'

He kissed her tenderly. 'At the moment, my darling, I'm likely to say yes to anything you ask. So purely for your father's sake I agree—but there's a condition,' he added sternly.

Eliza nodded, resigned. 'I thought there might be. Tell me the worst, then.'

'I'll put up with a double wedding, but I'm not sharing my honeymoon with anyone but you!'

Let
HARLEQUIN ROMANCE®
take you

BACK TO THE

Come to the Diamond B Ranch,
near Fawn Creek, Arizona.

Meet Seth Brody, rancher. *And* Janna Whitley, city girl.
He's one man who's hard to impress. And she's a woman
with a lot to prove.

Read THE TENDERFOOT by Patricia Knoll,
January's hilarious Back to the Ranch title!

Available wherever Harlequin books are sold.

When the only time you have for yourself is...

STOLEN *moments*™

Christmas is such a busy time—with shopping, decorating, writing cards, trimming trees, wrapping gifts....

When you do have a few *stolen moments* to call your own, treat yourself to a brand-new *short* novel. Relax with one of our Stocking Stuffers— or with all six!

Each STOLEN MOMENTS title
is a complete and original contemporary romance that's the perfect length for the busy woman of the nineties! Especially at Christmas...

And they make perfect **stocking stuffers**, too! (For your mother, grandmother, daughters, friends, co-workers, neighbors, aunts, cousins—all the other women in your life!)

Look for the STOLEN MOMENTS display in December

STOCKING STUFFERS:

HIS MISTRESS Carrie Alexander
DANIEL'S DECEPTION Marie DeWitt
SNOW ANGEL Isolde Evans
THE FAMILY MAN Danielle Kelly
THE LONE WOLF Ellen Rogers
MONTANA CHRISTMAS Lynn Russell

HSM2

 WORLDWIDE LIBRARY®

Make Christmas a truly
Romantic experience—with

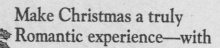 HARLEQUIN ROMANCE®

Wouldn't *you* love to kiss a tall, dark
Texan under the mistletoe? Gwen does,
in HOME FOR CHRISTMAS by
Ellen James. Share the experience!

Wouldn't *you* love to kiss a sexy
New Englander on a snowy Christmas
morning? Angela does, in Shannon
Waverly's CHRISTMAS ANGEL.
Share the experience!

Look for both of these Christmas
Romance titles, available in December
wherever Harlequin Books are sold.

(And don't forget that Romance novels
make great gifts! Easy to buy, easy to
wrap and just the right size for a
stocking stuffer. And they make a
wonderful treat when you need a break
from Christmas shopping, Christmas
wrapping and stuffing stockings!)

NEW YORK TIMES **Bestselling Author**

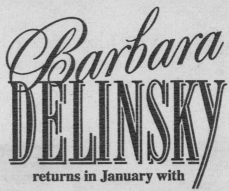

Barbara DELINSKY

returns in January with

The Real Thing

Stranded on an island off the coast of Maine,
Deirdre Joyce and Neil Hersey got the
solitude they so desperately craved—
but they also got each other, something they
hadn't expected. Nor had they expected
to be consumed by a desire so powerful
that the idea of living alone again was
unimaginable. A marrige of "convenience"
made sense—or did it? B0B7

 HARLEQUIN®